I0764300

Beowulf

Beowulf

Author unknown;
Translated by Gummere

Waking Lion Press

The views expressed in this book are the responsibility of the author and do not necessarily represent the position of The Editorium. The reader alone is responsible for the use of any ideas or information provided by this book.

This book is a work of fiction. The characters, places, and incidents in it are the products of the author's imagination or are represented fictitiously. Any resemblance of characters or events to actual persons or events is coincidental.

ISBN 978-1-4341-1524-9

Published by Waking Lion Press, an imprint of The Editorium

The Editorium, LLC
West Valley City, UT 84128-3917
wakinglionpress.com
wakinglion@editorium.com

Prelude of the Founder of the Danish House

LO, praise of the prowess of people-kings of spear-armed Danes, in days long sped, we have heard, and what honor the athelings won!

Oft Scyld the Scefing from squadroned foes, from many a tribe, the mead-bench tore, awing the earls. Since erst he lay friendless, a foundling, fate repaid him: for he waxed under welkin, in wealth he throve, till before him the folk, both far and near, who house by the whale-path, heard his mandate, gave him gifts: a good king he!

To him an heir was afterward born, a son in his halls, whom heaven sent to favor the folk, feeling their woe that erst they had lacked an earl for leader so long a while; the Lord endowed him, the Wielder of Wonder, with world's renown.

Famed was this Beowulf:[1] far flew the boast of him, son of Scyld, in the Scandian lands. So becomes it a youth to quit him well with his father's friends, by fee and gift, that to aid him, aged, in after days, come warriors willing, should war draw nigh, liegemen loyal: by lauded deeds shall an earl have honor in every clan.

1. Not, of course, Beowulf the Great, hero of the epic.

Forth he fared at the fated moment, sturdy Scyld to the shelter of God. Then they bore him over to ocean's billow, loving clansmen, as late he charged them, while wielded words the winsome Scyld, the leader beloved who long had ruled . . . In the roadstead rocked a ring-dight vessel, ice-flecked, outbound, atheling's barge: there laid they down their darling lord on the breast of the boat, the breaker-of-rings,[2] by the mast the mighty one.

Many a treasure fetched from far was freighted with him. No ship have I known so nobly dight with weapons of war and weeds of battle, with breastplate and blade: on his bosom lay a heaped hoard that hence should go far o'er the flood with him floating away. No less these loaded the lordly gifts, thanes' huge treasure, than those had done who in former time forth had sent him sole on the seas, a suckling child. High o'er his head they hoist the standard, a gold-wove banner; let billows take him, gave him to ocean.

Grave were their spirits, mournful their mood. No man is able to say in sooth, no son of the halls, no hero 'neath heaven,—who harbored that freight!

2. Kenning for king or chieftain of a comitatus: he breaks off gold from the spiral rings—often worn on the arm—and so rewards his followers.

I

Now Beowulf bode in the burg of the Scyldings, leader beloved, and long he ruled in fame with all folk, since his father had gone away from the world, till awoke an heir, haughty Healfdene, who held through life, sage and sturdy, the Scyldings glad.

Then, one after one, there woke to him, to the chieftain of clansmen, children four: Heorogar, then Hrothgar, then Halga brave; and I heard that —— was ——'s queen, the Heathoscylfing's helpmate dear.

To Hrothgar was given such glory of war, such honor of combat, that all his kin obeyed him gladly till great grew his band of youthful comrades. It came in his mind to bid his henchmen a hall uprear, a master mead-house, mightier far than ever was seen by the sons of earth, and within it, then, to old and young he would all allot that the Lord had sent him, save only the land and the lives of his men.

Wide, I heard, was the work commanded, for many a tribe this mid-earth round, to fashion the folkstead. It fell, as he ordered, in rapid achievement that ready it stood there, of halls the noblest:

Heorot[1] he named it whose message had might in many a land.

---

1. That is, "The Hart," or "Stag," so called from decorations in the

Not reckless of promise, the rings he dealt, treasure at banquet: there towered the hall, high, gabled wide, the hot surge waiting of furious flame.[2]

Nor far was that day when father and son-in-law stood in feud for warfare and hatred that woke again.[3]

With envy and anger an evil spirit endured the dole in his dark abode, that he heard each day the din of revel high in the hall: there harps rang out, clear song of the singer. He sang who knew[4] tales of the early time of man, how the Almighty made the earth, fairest fields enfolded by water, set, triumphant, sun and moon for a light to lighten the land-dwellers, and braided bright the breast

---

gables that resembled the antlers of a deer. This hall has been carefully described in a pamphlet by Heyne. The building was rectangular, with opposite doors—mainly west and east—and a hearth in the middle of the single room. A row of pillars down each side, at some distance from the walls, made a space which was raised a little above the main floor, and was furnished with two rows of seats.

On one side, usually south, was the high-seat midway between the doors. Opposite this, on the other raised space, was another seat of honor. At the banquet soon to be described, Hrothgar sat in the south or chief high-seat, and Beowulf opposite to him.

The scene for a flying (see below, v.499) was thus very effectively set. Planks on trestles—the "board" of later English literature—formed the tables just in front of the long rows of seats, and were taken away after banquets, when the retainers were ready to stretch themselves out for sleep on the benches.

2. Fire was the usual end of these halls. See v. 781 below. One thinks of the splendid scene at the end of the Nibelungen, of the Nialssaga, of Saxo's story of Amlethus, and many a less famous instance.

3. It is to be supposed that all hearers of this poem knew how Hrothgar's hall was burnt,—perhaps in the unsuccessful attack made on him by his son-in-law Ingeld.

4. A skilled minstrel. The Danes are heathens, as one is told presently; but this lay of beginnings is taken from Genesis.

of earth with limbs and leaves, made life for all of mortal beings that breathe and move. So lived the clansmen in cheer and revel a winsome life, till one began to fashion evils, that field of hell.

Grendel this monster grim was called, march-riever[5] mighty, in moorland living, in fen and fastness; fief of the giants the hapless wight a while had kept since the Creator his exile doomed.

On kin of Cain was the killing avenged by sovran God for slaughtered Abel. Ill fared his feud,[6] and far was he driven, for the slaughter's sake, from sight of men.

Of Cain awoke all that woful breed, Etins[7] and elves and evil-spirits, as well as the giants that warred with God weary while: but their wage was paid them!

---

5. A disturber of the border, one who sallies from his haunt in the fen and roams over the country near by. This probably pagan nuisance is now furnished with biblical credentials as a fiend or devil in good standing, so that all Christian Englishmen might read about him. "Grendel" may mean one who grinds and crushes.

6. Cain's.

7. Giants.

II

WENT he forth to find at fall of night that haughty house, and heed wherever the Ring-Danes, outrevelled, to rest had gone.

Found within it the atheling band asleep after feasting and fearless of sorrow, of human hardship.

Unhallowed wight, grim and greedy, he grasped betimes, wrathful, reckless, from resting-places, thirty of the thanes, and thence he rushed fain of his fell spoil, faring homeward, laden with slaughter, his lair to seek.

Then at the dawning, as day was breaking, the might of Grendel to men was known; then after wassail was wail uplifted, loud moan in the morn.

The mighty chief, atheling excellent, unblithe sat, labored in woe for the loss of his thanes, when once had been traced the trail of the fiend, spirit accurst: too cruel that sorrow, too long, too loathsome.

Not late the respite; with night returning, anew began ruthless murder; he recked no whit, firm in his guilt, of the feud and crime.

They were easy to find who elsewhere sought in room remote their rest at night, bed in the bowers,[1] when that

1. The smaller buildings within the main enclosure but separate from the hall.

bale was shown, was seen in sooth, with surest token,—the hall-thane's[2] hate.

Such held themselves far and fast who the fiend outran!

Thus ruled unrighteous and raged his fill one against all; until empty stood that lordly building, and long it bode so.

Twelve years' tide the trouble he bore, sovran of Scyldings, sorrows in plenty, boundless cares. There came unhidden tidings true to the tribes of men, in sorrowful songs, how ceaselessly Grendel harassed Hrothgar, what hate he bore him, what murder and massacre, many a year, feud unfading,—refused consent to deal with any of Daneland's earls, make pact of peace, or compound for gold: still less did the wise men ween to get great fee for the feud from his fiendish hands.

But the evil one ambushed old and young death-shadow dark, and dogged them still, lured, or lurked in the livelong night of misty moorlands: men may say not where the haunts of these Hell-Runes[3] be.

Such heaping of horrors the hater of men, lonely roamer, wrought unceasing, harassings heavy. O'er Heorot he lorded, gold-bright hall, in gloomy nights; and ne'er could the prince[4] approach his throne,—'twas judgment of God,—or have joy in his hall.

Sore was the sorrow to Scyldings'-friend, heart-rending misery. Many nobles sat assembled, and searched out counsel how it were best for bold-hearted men against harassing terror to try their hand. Whiles they vowed in

---

2. Grendel.
3. "Sorcerers-of-hell."
4. Hrothgar, who is the "Scyldings'-friend" of 170.

their heathen fanes altar-offerings, asked with words[5] that the slayer-of-souls would succor give them for the pain of their people. Their practice this, their heathen hope; 'twas Hell they thought of in mood of their mind.

Almighty they knew not, Doomsman of Deeds and dreadful Lord, nor Heaven's-Helmet heeded they ever, Wielder-of-Wonder.—Woe for that man who in harm and hatred hales his soul to fiery embraces;—nor favor nor change awaits he ever.

But well for him that after death-day may draw to his Lord, and friendship find in the Father's arms!

---

5. That is, in formal or prescribed phrase.

III

THUS seethed unceasing the son of Healfdene with the woe of these days; not wisest men assuaged his sorrow; too sore the anguish, loathly and long, that lay on his folk, most baneful of burdens and bales of the night.

This heard in his home Hygelac's thane, great among Geats, of Grendel's doings. He was the mightiest man of valor in that same day of this our life, stalwart and stately. A stout wave-walker he bade make ready.

Yon battle-king, said he, far o'er the swan-road he fain would seek, the noble monarch who needed men!

The prince's journey by prudent folk was little blamed, though they loved him dear; they whetted the hero, and hailed good omens.

And now the bold one from bands of Geats comrades chose, the keenest of warriors e'er he could find; with fourteen men the sea-wood[1] he sought, and, sailor proved, led them on to the land's confines.

Time had now flown;[2] afloat was the ship, boat under bluff. On board they climbed, warriors ready; waves were churning sea with sand; the sailors bore on the breast of the bark their bright array, their mail and weapons: the men pushed off, on its willing way, the well-braced craft.

1. Ship.
2. That is, since Beowulf selected his ship and led his men to the harbor.

Then moved o'er the waters by might of the wind that bark like a bird with breast of foam, till in season due, on the second day, the curved prow such course had run that sailors now could see the land, sea-cliffs shining, steep high hills, headlands broad. Their haven was found, their journey ended.

Up then quickly the Weders'[3] clansmen climbed ashore, anchored their sea-wood, with armor clashing and gear of battle: God they thanked or passing in peace o'er the paths of the sea.

Now saw from the cliff a Scylding clansman, a warden that watched the water-side, how they bore o'er the gangway glittering shields, war-gear in readiness; wonder seized him to know what manner of men they were.

Straight to the strand his steed he rode, Hrothgar's henchman; with hand of might he shook his spear, and spake in parley. "Who are ye, then, ye armed men, mailed folk, that yon mighty vessel have urged thus over the ocean ways, here o'er the waters? A warden I, sentinel set o'er the sea-march here, lest any foe to the folk of Danes with harrying fleet should harm the land.

No aliens ever at ease thus bore them, linden-wielders:[4] yet word-of-leave clearly ye lack from clansmen here, my folk's agreement.—A greater ne'er saw I of warriors in world than is one of you,—yon hero in harness! No henchman he worthied by weapons, if witness his features, his peerless presence! I pray you, though, tell your folk and home, lest hence ye fare suspect to wander your way as spies in Danish land.

---

3. One of the auxiliary names of the Geats.
4. Or: Not thus openly ever came warriors hither; yet . . .

Now, dwellers afar, ocean-travellers, take from me simple advice: the sooner the better I hear of the country whence ye came."

IV

To him the stateliest spake in answer; the warriors' leader his word-hoard unlocked:—"We are by kin of the clan of Geats, and Hygelac's own hearth-fellows we. To folk afar was my father known, noble atheling, Ecgtheow named. Full of winters, he fared away aged from earth; he is honored still through width of the world by wise men all. To thy lord and liege in loyal mood we hasten hither, to Healfdene's son, people-protector: be pleased to advise us!

To that mighty-one come we on mickle errand, to the lord of the Danes; nor deem I right that aught be hidden. We hear—thou knowest if sooth it is—the saying of men, that amid the Scyldings a scathing monster, dark ill-doer, in dusky nights shows terrific his rage unmatched, hatred and murder.

To Hrothgar I in greatness of soul would succor bring, so the Wise-and-Brave[1] may worst his foes,—if ever the end of ills is fated, of cruel contest, if cure shall follow, and the boiling care-waves cooler grow; else ever afterward anguish-days he shall suffer in sorrow while stands in place high on its hill that house unpeered!"

Astride his steed, the strand-ward answered, clansman unquailing: "The keen-souled thane must be skilled to

1. Hrothgar.

sever and sunder duly words and works, if he well intends. I gather, this band is graciously bent to the Scyldings' master. March, then, bearing weapons and weeds the way I show you. I will bid my men your boat meanwhile to guard for fear lest foemen come,—your new-tarred ship by shore of ocean faithfully watching till once again it waft o'er the waters those well-loved thanes,—winding-neck'd wood,—to Weders' bounds, heroes such as the hest of fate shall succor and save from the shock of war."

They bent them to march,—the boat lay still, fettered by cable and fast at anchor, broad-bosomed ship.—Then shone the boars[2] over the cheek-guard; chased with gold, keen and gleaming, guard it kept o'er the man of war, as marched along heroes in haste, till the hall they saw, broad of gable and bright with gold: that was the fairest, 'mid folk of earth, of houses 'neath heaven, where Hrothgar lived, and the gleam of it lightened o'er lands afar.

The sturdy shieldsman showed that bright burg-of-the-boldest; bade them go straightway thither; his steed then turned, hardy hero, and hailed them thus:—

"Tis time that I fare from you. Father Almighty in grace and mercy guard you well, safe in your seekings. Seaward I go, 'gainst hostile warriors hold my watch."

---

2. Beowulf's helmet has several boar-images on it; he is the "man of war"; and the boar-helmet guards him as typical representative of the marching party as a whole. The boar was sacred to Freyr, who was the favorite god of the Germanic tribes about the North Sea and the Baltic. Rude representations of warriors show the boar on the helmet quite as large as the helmet itself.

V

STONE-BRIGHT the street:[1] it showed the way to the crowd of clansmen.

Corselets glistened hand-forged, hard; on their harness bright the steel ring sang, as they strode along in mail of battle, and marched to the hall.

There, weary of ocean, the wall along they set their bucklers, their broad shields, down, and bowed them to bench: the breastplates clanged, war-gear of men; their weapons stacked, spears of the seafarers stood together, gray-tipped ash: that iron band was worthily weaponed!—

A warrior proud asked of the heroes their home and kin. "Whence, now, bear ye burnished shields, harness gray and helmets grim, spears in multitude? Messenger, I, Hrothgar's herald! Heroes so many ne'er met I as strangers of mood so strong. 'Tis plain that for prowess, not plunged into exile, for high-hearted valor, Hrothgar ye seek!"

Him the sturdy-in-war bespake with words, proud earl of the Weders answer made, hardy 'neath helmet:—

"Hygelac's, we, fellows at board; I am Beowulf named. I am seeking to say to the son of Healfdene this mission of

---

1. Either merely paved, the strata via of the Romans, or else thought of as a sort of mosaic, an extravagant touch like the reckless waste of gold on the walls and roofs of a hall.

mine, to thy master-lord, the doughty prince, if he deign at all grace that we greet him, the good one, now."

Wulfgar spake, the Wendles' chieftain, whose might of mind to many was known, his courage and counsel: "The king of Danes, the Scyldings' friend, I fain will tell, the Breaker-of-Rings, as the boon thou askest, the famed prince, of thy faring hither, and, swiftly after, such answer bring as the doughty monarch may deign to give."

Hied then in haste to where Hrothgar sat white-haired and old, his earls about him, till the stout thane stood at the shoulder there of the Danish king: good courtier he!

Wulfgar spake to his winsome lord:—

"Hither have fared to thee far-come men o'er the paths of ocean, people of Geatland; and the stateliest there by his sturdy band is Beowulf named. This boon they seek, that they, my master, may with thee have speech at will: nor spurn their prayer to give them hearing, gracious Hrothgar! In weeds of the warrior worthy they, methinks, of our liking; their leader most surely, a hero that hither his henchmen has led."

VI

HROTHGAR answered, helmet of Scyldings:—

"I knew him of yore in his youthful days; his aged father was Ecgtheow named, to whom, at home, gave Hrethel the Geat his only daughter. Their offspring bold fares hither to seek the steadfast friend. And seamen, too, have said me this,—who carried my gifts to the Geatish court, thither for thanks,—he has thirty men's heft of grasp in the gripe of his hand, the bold-in-battle.

Blessed God out of his mercy this man hath sent to Danes of the West, as I ween indeed, against horror of Grendel.

I hope to give the good youth gold for his gallant thought. Be thou in haste, and bid them hither, clan of kinsmen, to come before me; and add this word,—they are welcome guests to folk of the Danes."

[To the door of the hall Wulfgar went] and the word declared:—

"To you this message my master sends, East-Danes' king, that your kin he knows, hardy heroes, and hails you all welcome hither o'er waves of the sea!

Ye may wend your way in war-attire, and under helmets Hrothgar greet; but let here the battle-shields bide your parley, and wooden war-shafts wait its end."

Uprose the mighty one, ringed with his men, brave band of thanes: some bode without, battle-gear guarding, as bade the chief.

Then hied that troop where the herald led them, under Heorot's roof: [the hero strode,] hardy 'neath helm, till the hearth he neared.

Beowulf spake,—his breastplate gleamed, war-net woven by wit of the smith:—

"Thou Hrothgar, hail! Hygelac's I, kinsman and follower. Fame a plenty have I gained in youth! These Grendel-deeds I heard in my home-land heralded clear. Seafarers say how stands this hall, of buildings best, for your band of thanes empty and idle, when evening sun in the harbor of heaven is hidden away.

So my vassals advised me well,—brave and wise, the best of men,—O sovran Hrothgar, to seek thee here, for my nerve and my might they knew full well. Themselves had seen me from slaughter come blood-flecked from foes, where five I bound, and that wild brood worsted.

I' the waves I slew nicors[1] by night, in need and peril avenging the Weders,[2] whose woe they sought,—crushing the grim ones.

Grendel now, monster cruel, be mine to quell in single battle!

So, from thee, thou sovran of the Shining-Danes, Scyldings'-bulwark, a boon I seek,—and, Friend-of-the-folk,

---

1. The nicor, says Bugge, is a hippopotamus; a walrus, says ten Brink. But that water-goblin who covers the space from Old Nick of jest to the Neckan and Nix of poetry and tale, is all one needs, and Nicor is a good name for him.

2. His own people, the Geats.

refuse it not, O Warriors'-shield, now I've wandered far,—that I alone with my liegemen here, this hardy band, may Heorot purge!

More I hear, that the monster dire, in his wanton mood, of weapons recks not; hence shall I scorn—so Hygelac stay, king of my kindred, kind to me!—brand or buckler to bear in the fight, gold-colored targe: but with gripe alone must I front the fiend and fight for life, foe against foe.

Then faith be his in the doom of the Lord whom death shall take. Fain, I ween, if the fight he win, in this hall of gold my Geatish band will he fearless eat,—as oft before,—my noblest thanes.

Nor need'st thou then to hide my head;[3] for his shall I be, dyed in gore, if death must take me; and my blood-covered body he'll bear as prey, ruthless devour it, the roamer-lonely, with my life-blood redden his lair in the fen: no further for me need'st food prepare!

To Hygelac send, if Hild[4] should take me, best of war-weeds, warding my breast, armor excellent, heirloom of Hrethel and work of Wayland.[5] Fares Wyrd[6] as she must."

---

3. That is, cover it as with a face-cloth. "There will be no need of funeral rites."

4. Personification of Battle.

5. The Germanic Vulcan.

6. This mighty power, whom the Christian poet can still revere, has here the general force of "Destiny."

VII

HROTHGAR spake, the Scyldings'-helmet:—

"For fight defensive, Friend my Beowulf, to succor and save, thou hast sought us here. Thy father's combat[1] a feud enkindled when Heatholaf with hand he slew among the Wylfings; his Weder kin for horror of fighting feared to hold him.

Fleeing, he sought our South-Dane folk, over surge of ocean the Honor-Scyldings, when first I was ruling the folk of Danes, wielded, youthful, this widespread realm, this hoard-hold of heroes.

Heorogar was dead, my elder brother, had breathed his last, Healfdene's bairn: he was better than I!

Straightway the feud with fee[2] I settled, to the Wylfings sent, o'er watery ridges, treasures olden: oaths he[3] swore me.

Sore is my soul to say to any of the race of man what ruth for me in Heorot Grendel with hate hath wrought, what sudden harryings. Hall-folk fail me, my warriors wane; for Wyrd hath swept them into Grendel's grasp.

---

1. There is no irrelevance here. Hrothgar sees in Beowulf's mission a heritage of duty, a return of the good offices which the Danish king rendered to Beowulf's father in time of dire need.

2. Money, for wergild, or man-price.

3. Ecgtheow, Beowulf's sire.

But God is able this deadly foe from his deeds to turn! Boasted full oft, as my beer they drank, earls o'er the ale-cup, armed men, that they would bide in the beer-hall here, Grendel's attack with terror of blades.

Then was this mead-house at morning tide dyed with gore, when the daylight broke, all the boards of the benches blood-besprinkled, gory the hall: I had heroes the less, doughty dear-ones that death had reft.

But sit to the banquet, unbind thy words, hardy hero, as heart shall prompt thee."

Gathered together, the Geatish men in the banquet-hall on bench assigned, sturdy-spirited, sat them down, hardy-hearted. A henchman attended, carried the carven cup in hand, served the clear mead.

Oft minstrels sang blithe in Heorot. Heroes revelled, no dearth of warriors, Weder and Dane.

VIII

UNFERTH spake, the son of Ecglaf, who sat at the feet of the Scyldings' lord, unbound the battle-runes.[1] Beowulf's quest, sturdy seafarer's, sorely galled him; ever he envied that other men should more achieve in middle-earth of fame under heaven than he himself.—

"Art thou that Beowulf, Breca's rival, who emulous swam on the open sea, when for pride the pair of you proved the floods, and wantonly dared in waters deep to risk your lives? No living man, or lief or loath, from your labor dire could you dissuade, from swimming the main.

Ocean-tides with your arms ye covered, with strenuous hands the sea-streets measured, swam o'er the waters. Winter's storm rolled the rough waves. In realm of sea a sennight strove ye.

In swimming he topped thee, had more of main! Him at morning-tide billows bore to the Battling Reamas, whence he hied to his home so dear beloved of his liegemen, to land of Brondings, fastness fair, where his folk he ruled, town and treasure.

In triumph o'er thee Beanstan's bairn[2] his boast achieved.

So ween I for thee a worse adventure—though in buffet of battle thou brave hast been, in struggle grim,—if

1. "Began the fight."

2. Breca.

Grendel's approach thou darst await through the watch of night!"

Beowulf spake, bairn of Ecgtheow:—

"What a deal hast uttered, dear my Unferth, drunken with beer, of Breca now, told of his triumph!

Truth I claim it, that I had more of might in the sea than any man else, more ocean-endurance.

We twain had talked, in time of youth, and made our boast,—we were merely boys, striplings still,—to stake our lives far at sea: and so we performed it. Naked swords, as we swam along, we held in hand, with hope to guard us against the whales.

Not a whit from me could he float afar o'er the flood of waves, haste o'er the billows; nor him I abandoned.

Together we twain on the tides abode five nights full till the flood divided us, churning waves and chillest weather, darkling night, and the northern wind ruthless rushed on us: rough was the surge.

Now the wrath of the sea-fish rose apace; yet me 'gainst the monsters my mailed coat, hard and hand-linked, help afforded,—battle-sark braided my breast to ward, garnished with gold.

There grasped me firm and haled me to bottom the hated foe, with grimmest gripe. 'Twas granted me, though, to pierce the monster with point of sword, with blade of battle: huge beast of the sea was whelmed by the hurly through hand of mine.

IX

ME thus often the evil monsters thronging threatened. With thrust of my sword, the darling, I dealt them due return!

Nowise had they bliss from their booty then to devour their victim, vengeful creatures, seated to banquet at bottom of sea; but at break of day, by my brand sore hurt, on the edge of ocean up they lay, put to sleep by the sword.

And since, by them on the fathomless sea-ways sailor-folk are never molested.—Light from east, came bright God's beacon; the billows sank, so that I saw the sea-cliffs high, windy walls.

For Wyrd oft saveth earl undoomed if he doughty be!

And so it came that I killed with my sword nine of the nicors. Of night-fought battles ne'er heard I a harder 'neath heaven's dome, nor adrift on the deep a more desolate man!

Yet I came unharmed from that hostile clutch, though spent with swimming. The sea upbore me, flood of the tide, on Finnish land, the welling waters.

No wise of thee have I heard men tell such terror of falchions, bitter battle. Breca ne'er yet, not one of you pair, in the play of war such daring deed has done at all with bloody brand,—I boast not of it!—though thou wast the bane[1] of thy brethren dear, thy closest kin, whence curse of hell awaits thee, well as thy wit may serve!

For I say in sooth, thou son of Ecglaf, never had Grendel these grim deeds wrought, monster dire, on thy master dear, in Heorot such havoc, if heart of thine were as battle-bold as thy boast is loud!

But he has found no feud will happen; from sword-clash dread of your Danish clan he vaunts him safe, from the Victor-Scyldings.

He forces pledges, favors none of the land of Danes, but lustily murders, fights and feasts, nor feud he dreads from Spear-Dane men.

But speedily now shall I prove him the prowess and pride of the Geats, shall bid him battle.

Blithe to mead go he that listeth, when light of dawn this morrow morning o'er men of earth, ether-robed sun from the south shall beam!"

Joyous then was the Jewel-giver, hoar-haired, war-brave; help awaited the Bright-Danes' prince, from Beowulf hearing, folk's good shepherd, such firm resolve.

Then was laughter of liegemen loud resounding with winsome words. Came Wealhtheow forth, queen of Hrothgar, heedful of courtesy, gold-decked, greeting the guests in hall; and the high-born lady handed the cup first to the East-Danes' heir and warden, bade him be blithe at the beer-carouse, the land's beloved one.

Lustily took he banquet and beaker, battle-famed king.

Through the hall then went the Helmings' Lady, to younger and older everywhere carried the cup, till come the moment when the ring-graced queen, the royal-hearted to Beowulf bore the beaker of mead.

---

1. Murder.

She greeted the Geats' lord, God she thanked, in wisdom's words, that her will was granted, that at last on a hero her hope could lean for comfort in terrors.

The cup he took, hardy-in-war, from Wealhtheow's hand, and answer uttered the eager-for-combat.

Beowulf spake, bairn of Ecgtheow:—

"This was my thought, when my thanes and I bent to the ocean and entered our boat, that I would work the will of your people fully, or fighting fall in death, in fiend's gripe fast. I am firm to do an earl's brave deed, or end the days of this life of mine in the mead-hall here."

Well these words to the woman seemed, Beowulf's battle-boast.—Bright with gold the stately dame by her spouse sat down.

Again, as erst, began in hall warriors' wassail and words of power, the proud-band's revel, till presently the son of Healfdene hastened to seek rest for the night; he knew there waited fight for the fiend in that festal hall, when the sheen of the sun they saw no more, and dusk of night sank darkling nigh, and shadowy shapes came striding on, wan under welkin.

The warriors rose. Man to man, he made harangue, Hrothgar to Beowulf, bade him hail, let him wield the wine hall: a word he added:—

"Never to any man erst I trusted, since I could heave up hand and shield, this noble Dane-Hall, till now to thee. Have now and hold this house unpeered; remember thy glory; thy might declare; watch for the foe!

No wish shall fail thee if thou bidest the battle with bold-won life."

X

THEN Hrothgar went with his hero-train, defence-of-Scyldings, forth from hall; fain would the war-lord Wealhtheow seek, couch of his queen.

The King-of-Glory against this Grendel a guard had set, so heroes heard, a hall-defender, who warded the monarch and watched for the monster.

In truth, the Geats' prince gladly trusted his mettle, his might, the mercy of God!

Cast off then his corselet of iron, helmet from head; to his henchman gave,—choicest of weapons,—the well-chased sword, bidding him guard the gear of battle.

Spake then his Vaunt the valiant man, Beowulf Geat, ere the bed be sought:—

"Of force in fight no feebler I count me, in grim war-deeds, than Grendel deems him. Not with the sword, then, to sleep of death his life will I give, though it lie in my power. No skill is his to strike against me, my shield to hew though he hardy be, bold in battle; we both, this night, shall spurn the sword, if he seek me here, unweaponed, for war. Let wisest God, sacred Lord, on which side soever doom decree as he deemeth right."

Reclined then the chieftain, and cheek-pillows held the head of the earl, while all about him seamen hardy on hall-beds sank.

None of them thought that thence their steps to the folk and fastness that fostered them, to the land they loved, would lead them back! Full well they wist that on warriors many battle-death seized, in the banquet-hall, of Danish clan.

But comfort and help, war-weal weaving, to Weder folk the Master gave, that, by might of one, over their enemy all prevailed, by single strength.

In sooth 'tis told that highest God o'er human kind hath wielded ever!—Thro' wan night striding, came the walker-in-shadow.

Warriors slept whose hest was to guard the gabled hall,—all save one. 'Twas widely known that against God's will the ghostly ravager him[1] could not hurl to haunts of darkness; wakeful, ready, with warrior's wrath, bold he bided the battle's issue.

1. Beowulf,—the "one."

XI

THEN from the moorland, by misty crags, with God's wrath laden, Grendel came.

The monster was minded of mankind now sundry to seize in the stately house.

Under welkin he walked, till the wine-palace there, gold-hall of men, he gladly discerned, flashing with fretwork. Not first time, this, that he the home of Hrothgar sought,—yet ne'er in his life-day, late or early, such hardy heroes, such hall-thanes, found!

To the house the warrior walked apace, parted from peace;[1] the portal opended, though with forged bolts fast, when his fists had struck it, and baleful he burst in his blatant rage, the house's mouth.

All hastily, then, o'er fair-paved floor the fiend trod on, ireful he strode; there streamed from his eyes fearful flashes, like flame to see.

He spied in hall the hero-band, kin and clansmen clustered asleep, hardy liegemen. Then laughed his heart; for the monster was minded, ere morn should dawn, savage, to sever the soul of each, life from body, since lusty banquet waited his will!

But Wyrd forbade him to seize any more of men on earth after that evening.

---

1. That is, he was a "lost soul," doomed to hell.

Eagerly watched Hygelac's kinsman his cursed foe, how he would fare in fell attack. Not that the monster was minded to pause!

Straightway he seized a sleeping warrior for the first, and tore him fiercely asunder, the bone-frame bit, drank blood in streams, swallowed him piecemeal: swiftly thus the lifeless corse was clear devoured, e'en feet and hands.

Then farther he hied; for the hardy hero with hand he grasped, felt for the foe with fiendish claw, for the hero reclining,—who clutched it boldly, prompt to answer, propped on his arm.

Soon then saw that shepherd-of-evils that never he met in this middle-world, in the ways of earth, another wight with heavier hand-gripe; at heart he feared, sorrowed in soul,—none the sooner escaped!

Fain would he flee, his fastness seek, the den of devils: no doings now such as oft he had done in days of old!

Then bethought him the hardy Hygelac-thane of his boast at evening: up he bounded, grasped firm his foe, whose fingers cracked.

The fiend made off, but the earl close followed. The monster meant—if he might at all—to fling himself free, and far away fly to the fens,—knew his fingers' power in the gripe of the grim one.

Gruesome march to Heorot this monster of harm had made! Din filled the room; the Danes were bereft, castle-dwellers and clansmen all, earls, of their ale. Angry were both those savage hall-guards: the house resounded.

Wonder it was the wine-hall firm in the strain of their struggle stood, to earth the fair house fell not; too fast it was within and without by its iron bands craftily clamped; though there crashed from sill many a mead-bench—men have told me—gay with gold, where the grim foes wrestled.

So well had weened the wisest Scyldings that not ever at all might any man that bone-decked, brave house break asunder, crush by craft,—unless clasp of fire in smoke engulfed it.—Again uprose din redoubled.

Danes of the North with fear and frenzy were filled, each one, who from the wall that wailing heard, God's foe sounding his grisly song, cry of the conquered, clamorous pain from captive of hell. Too closely held him he who of men in might was strongest in that same day of this our life.

XII

NOT in any wise would the earls'-defence[1] suffer that slaughterous stranger to live, useless deeming his days and years to men on earth.

Now many an earl of Beowulf brandished blade ancestral, fain the life of their lord to shield, their praised prince, if power were theirs; never they knew,—as they neared the foe, hardy-hearted heroes of war, aiming their swords on every side the accursed to kill,—no keenest blade, no farest of falchions fashioned on earth, could harm or hurt that hideous fiend!

He was safe, by his spells, from sword of battle, from edge of iron. Yet his end and parting on that same day of this our life woful should be, and his wandering soul far off flit to the fiends' domain.

Soon he found, who in former days, harmful in heart and hated of God, on many a man such murder wrought, that the frame of his body failed him now. For him the keen-souled kinsman of Hygelac held in hand; hateful alive was each to other.

The outlaw dire took mortal hurt; a mighty wound showed on his shoulder, and sinews cracked, and the bone-frame burst.

1. Kenning for Beowulf.

To Beowulf now the glory was given, and Grendel thence death-sick his den in the dark moor sought, noisome abode: he knew too well that here was the last of life, an end of his days on earth.—To all the Danes by that bloody battle the boon had come.

From ravage had rescued the roving stranger Hrothgar's hall; the hardy and wise one had purged it anew.

His night-work pleased him, his deed and its honor. To Eastern Danes had the valiant Geat his vaunt made good, all their sorrow and ills assuaged, their bale of battle borne so long, and all the dole they erst endured pain a-plenty. Twas proof of this, when the hardy-in-fight a hand laid down, arm and shoulder,—all, indeed, of Grendel's gripe,—'neath the gabled roof.

XIII

MANY at morning, as men have told me, warriors gathered the gift-hall round, folk-leaders faring from far and near, o'er wide-stretched ways, the wonder to view, trace of the traitor.

Not troublous seemed the enemy's end to any man who saw by the gait of the graceless foe how the weary-hearted, away from thence, baffled in battle and banned, his steps death-marked dragged to the devils' mere.

Bloody the billows were boiling there, turbid the tide of tumbling waves horribly seething, with sword-blood hot, by that doomed one dyed, who in den of the moor laid forlorn his life adown, his heathen soul, and hell received it.

Home then rode the hoary clansmen from that merry journey, and many a youth, on horses white, the hardy warriors, back from the mere.

Then Beowulf's glory eager they echoed, and all averred that from sea to sea, or south or north, there was no other in earth's domain, under vault of heaven, more valiant found, of warriors none more worthy to rule! (On their lord beloved they laid no slight, gracious Hrothgar: a good king he!)

From time to time, the tried-in-battle their gray steeds set to gallop amain, and ran a race when the road seemed fair. From time to time, a thane of the king, who had made many vaunts, and was mindful of verses, stored with sagas and songs of old, bound word to word in well-knit rime, welded his lay; this warrior soon of Beowulf's quest right cleverly sang, and artfully added an excellent tale, in well-ranged words, of the warlike deeds he had heard in saga of Sigemund.

Strange the story: he said it all,—the Waelsing's wanderings wide, his struggles, which never were told to tribes of men, the feuds and the frauds, save to Fitela only, when of these doings he deigned to speak, uncle to nephew; as ever the twain stood side by side in stress of war, and multitude of the monster kind they had felled with their swords.

Of Sigemund grew, when he passed from life, no little praise; for the doughty-in-combat a dragon killed that herded the hoard:[1] under hoary rock the atheling dared the deed alone fearful quest, nor was Fitela there.

Yet so it befell, his falchion pierced that wondrous worm,—on the wall it struck, best blade; the dragon died in its blood.

Thus had the dread-one by daring achieved over the ring-hoard to rule at will, himself to pleasure; a sea-boat he loaded, and bore on its bosom the beaming gold, son of Waels; the worm was consumed.

He had of all heroes the highest renown among races of men, this refuge-of-warriors, for deeds of daring that decked his name since the hand and heart of Heremod grew slack in battle.

He, swiftly banished to mingle with monsters at mercy of foes, to death was betrayed; for torrents of sorrow had

1. "Guarded the treasure."

lamed him too long; a load of care to earls and athelings all he proved.

Oft indeed, in earlier days, for the warrior's wayfaring wise men mourned, who had hoped of him help from harm and bale, and had thought their sovran's son would thrive, follow his father, his folk protect, the hoard and the stronghold, heroes' land, home of Scyldings.—But here, thanes said, the kinsman of Hygelac kinder seemed to all: the other[2] was urged to crime!

And afresh to the race,[3] the fallow roads by swift steeds measured! The morning sun was climbing higher. Clansmen hastened to the high-built hall, those hardy-minded, the wonder to witness.

Warden of treasure, crowned with glory, the king himself, with stately band from the bride-bower strode; and with him the queen and her crowd of maidens measured the path to the mead-house fair.

---

2. Sc. Heremod.

3. The singer has sung his lays, and the epic resumes its story. The time-relations are not altogether good in this long passage which describes the rejoicings of "the day after"; but the present shift from the riders on the road to the folk at the hall is not very violent, and is of a piece with the general style.

XIV

HROTHGAR spake,—to the hall he went, stood by the steps, the steep roof saw, garnished with gold, and Grendel's hand:—

"For the sight I see to the Sovran Ruler be speedy thanks! A throng of sorrows I have borne from Grendel; but God still works wonder on wonder, the Warden-of-Glory.

It was but now that I never more for woes that weighed on me waited help long as I lived, when, laved in blood, stood sword-gore-stained this stateliest house,—widespread woe for wise men all, who had no hope to hinder ever foes infernal and fiendish sprites from havoc in hall.

This hero now, by the Wielder's might, a work has done that not all of us erst could ever do by wile and wisdom.

Lo, well can she say whoso of women this warrior bore among sons of men, if still she liveth, that the God of the ages was good to her in the birth of her bairn.

Now, Beowulf, thee, of heroes best, I shall heartily love as mine own, my son; preserve thou ever this kinship new: thou shalt never lack wealth of the world that I wield as mine!

Full oft for less have I largess showered, my precious hoard, on a punier man, less stout in struggle. Thyself hast now fulfilled such deeds, that thy fame shall endure through all the ages.

As ever he did, well may the Wielder reward thee still!"

Beowulf spake, bairn of Ecgtheow:—

"This work of war most willingly we have fought, this fight, and fearlessly dared force of the foe. Fain, too, were I hadst thou but seen himself, what time the fiend in his trappings tottered to fall!

Swiftly, I thought, in strongest gripe on his bed of death to bind him down, that he in the hent of this hand of mine should breathe his last: but he broke away.

Him I might not—the Maker willed not—hinder from flight, and firm enough hold the life-destroyer: too sturdy was he, the ruthless, in running!

For rescue, however, he left behind him his hand in pledge, arm and shoulder; nor aught of help could the cursed one thus procure at all.

None the longer liveth he, loathsome fiend, sunk in his sins, but sorrow holds him tightly grasped in gripe of anguish, in baleful bonds, where bide he must, evil outlaw, such awful doom as the Mighty Maker shall mete him out."

More silent seemed the son of Ecglaf[1] in boastful speech of his battle-deeds, since athelings all, through the earl's great prowess, beheld that hand, on the high roof gazing, foeman's fingers,—the forepart of each of the sturdy nails to steel was likest,—heathen's "hand-spear," hostile warrior's claw uncanny.

'Twas clear, they said, that him no blade of the brave could touch, how keen soever, or cut away that battle-hand bloody from baneful foe.

---

1. Unferth, Beowulf's sometime opponent in the flyting.

XV

THERE was hurry and hest in Heorot now for hands to bedeck it, and dense was the throng of men and women the wine-hall to cleanse, the guest-room to garnish. Gold-gay shone the hangings that were wove on the wall, and wonders many to delight each mortal that looks upon them.

Though braced within by iron bands, that building bright was broken sorely;[1] rent were its hinges; the roof alone held safe and sound, when, seared with crime, the fiendish foe his flight essayed, of life despairing.—No light thing that, the flight for safety,—essay it who will!

Forced of fate, he shall find his way to the refuge ready for race of man, for soul-possessors, and sons of earth; and there his body on bed of death shall rest after revel.

Arrived was the hour when to hall proceeded Healfdene's son: the king himself would sit to banquet. Ne'er heard I of host in haughtier throng more graciously gathered round giver-of-rings!

Bowed then to bench those bearers-of-glory, fain of the feasting. Featly received many a mead-cup the mighty-in-

---

1. There is no horrible inconsistency here such as the critics strive and cry about. In spite of the ruin that Grendel and Beowulf had made within the hall, the framework and roof held firm, and swift repairs made the interior habitable. Tapestries were hung on the walls, and willing hands prepared the banquet.

spirit, kinsmen who sat in the sumptuous hall, Hrothgar and Hrothulf.

Heorot now was filled with friends; the folk of Scyldings ne'er yet had tried the traitor's deed.

To Beowulf gave the bairn of Healfdene a gold-wove banner, guerdon of triumph, broidered battle-flag, breastplate and helmet; and a splendid sword was seen of many borne to the brave one.

Beowulf took cup in hall:[2] for such costly gifts he suffered no shame in that soldier throng. For I heard of few heroes, in heartier mood, with four such gifts, so fashioned with gold, on the ale-bench honoring others thus!

O'er the roof of the helmet high, a ridge, wound with wires, kept ward o'er the head, lest the relict-of-files[3] should fierce invade, sharp in the strife, when that shielded hero should go to grapple against his foes.

Then the earls'-defence[4] on the floor[5] bade lead coursers eight, with carven head-gear, adown the hall: one horse was decked with a saddle all shining and set in jewels; 'twas the battle-seat of the best of kings, when to play of swords the son of Healfdene was fain to fare. Ne'er failed his valor in the crush of combat when corpses fell.

To Beowulf over them both then gave the refuge-of-Ingwines right and power, o'er war-steeds and weapons:

---

2. From its formal use in other places, this phrase, to take cup in hall, or "on the floor," would seem to mean that Beowulf stood up to receive his gifts, drink to the donor, and say thanks.

3. Kenning for sword.

4. Hrothgar. He is also the "refuge of the friends of Ing," below. Ing belongs to myth.

5. Horses are frequently led or ridden into the hall where folk sit at banquet: so in Chaucer's Squire's tale, in the ballad of King Estmere, and in the romances.

wished him joy of them. Manfully thus the mighty prince, hoard-guard for heroes, that hard fight repaid with steeds and treasures contemned by none who is willing to say the sooth aright.

XVI

AND the lord of earls, to each that came with Beowulf over the briny ways, an heirloom there at the ale-bench gave, precious gift; and the price[1] bade pay in gold for him whom Grendel erst murdered,—and fain of them more had killed, had not wisest God their Wyrd averted, and the man's[2] brave mood.

The Maker then ruled human kind, as here and now. Therefore is insight always best, and forethought of mind.

How much awaits him of lief and of loath, who long time here, through days of warfare this world endures! Then song and music mingled sounds in the presence of Healfdene's head-of-armies[3] and harping was heard with the hero-lay as Hrothgar's singer the hall-joy woke along the mead-seats, making his song of that sudden raid on the sons of Finn.[4]

---

1. Man-price, wergild.
2. Beowulf's.
3. Hrothgar.
4. There is no need to assume a gap in the Ms. As before about Sigemund and Heremod, so now, though at greater length, about Finn and his feud, a lay is chanted or recited; and the epic poet, counting on his readers' familiarity with the story,—a fragment of it still exists,—simply gives the headings.

Healfdene's hero, Hnaef the Scylding, was fated to fall in the Frisian slaughter.[5]

Hildeburh needed not hold in value her enemies' honor![6] Innocent both were the loved ones she lost at the linden-play, bairn and brother, they bowed to fate, stricken by spears; 'twas a sorrowful woman!

None doubted why the daughter of Hoc bewailed her doom when dawning came, and under the sky she saw them lying, kinsmen murdered, where most she had kenned of the sweets of the world!

By war were swept, too, Finn's own liegemen, and few were left; in the parleying-place[7] he could ply no longer weapon, nor war could he wage on Hengest, and rescue his remnant by right of arms from the prince's thane.

A pact he offered: another dwelling the Danes should have, hall and high-seat, and half the power should fall to them in Frisian land; and at the fee-gifts, Folcwald's son

---

5. The exact story to which this episode refers in summary is not to be determined, but the following account of it is reasonable and has good support among scholars. Finn, a Frisian chieftain, who nevertheless has a "castle" outside the Frisian border, marries Hildeburh, a Danish princess; and her brother, Hnaef, with many other Danes, pays Finn a visit. Relations between the two peoples have been strained before. Something starts the old feud anew; and the visitors are attacked in their quarters. Hnaef is killed; so is a son of Hildeburh. Many fall on both sides. Peace is patched up; a stately funeral is held; and the surviving visitors become in a way vassals or liegemen of Finn, going back with him to Frisia. So matters rest a while. Hengest is now leader of the Danes; but he is set upon revenge for his former lord, Hnaef. Probably he is killed in feud; but his clansmen, Guthlaf and Oslaf, gather at their home a force of sturdy Danes, come back to Frisia, storm Finn's stronghold, kill him, and carry back their kinswoman Hildeburh.

6. The "enemies" must be the Frisians.

7. Battlefield.—Hengest is the "prince's thane," companion of Hnaef. "Folcwald's son" is Finn.

day by day the Danes should honor, the folk of Hengest favor with rings, even as truly, with treasure and jewels, with fretted gold, as his Frisian kin he meant to honor in ale-hall there.

Pact of peace they plighted further on both sides firmly. Finn to Hengest with oath, upon honor, openly promised that woful remnant, with wise-men's aid, nobly to govern, so none of the guests by word or work should warp the treaty,[8] or with malice of mind bemoan themselves as forced to follow their fee-giver's slayer, lordless men, as their lot ordained.

Should Frisian, moreover, with foeman's taunt, that murderous hatred to mind recall, then edge of the sword must seal his doom.

Oaths were given, and ancient gold heaped from hoard.— The hardy Scylding, battle-thane best,[9] on his balefire lay.

All on the pyre were plain to see the gory sark, the gilded swine-crest, boar of hard iron, and athelings many slain by the sword: at the slaughter they fell.

It was Hildeburh's hest, at Hnaef's own pyre the bairn of her body on brands to lay, his bones to burn, on the balefire placed, at his uncle's side. In sorrowful dirges bewept them the woman: great wailing ascended.

Then wound up to welkin the wildest of death-fires, roared o'er the hillock:[10] heads all were melted, gashes burst, and blood gushed out from bites[11] of the body. Bale-

---

8. That is, Finn would govern in all honor the few Danish warriors who were left, provided, of course, that none of them tried to renew the quarrel or avenge Hnaef their fallen lord. If, again, one of Finn's Frisians began a quarrel, he should die by the sword.

9. Hnaef.

10. The high place chosen for the funeral: see description of Beowulf's funeral-pile at the end of the poem.

11. Wounds.

fire devoured, greediest spirit, those spared not by war out of either folk: their flower was gone.

XVII

THEN hastened those heroes their home to see, friendless, to find the Frisian land, houses and high burg.

Hengest still through the death-dyed winter dwelt with Finn, holding pact, yet of home he minded, though powerless his ring-decked prow to drive over the waters, now waves rolled fierce lashed by the winds, or winter locked them in icy fetters.

Then fared another year to men's dwellings, as yet they do, the sunbright skies, that their season ever duly await. Far off winter was driven; fair lay earth's breast; and fain was the rover, the guest, to depart, though more gladly he pondered on wreaking his vengeance than roaming the deep, and how to hasten the hot encounter where sons of the Frisians were sure to be.

So he escaped not the common doom, when Hun with "Lafing," the light-of-battle, best of blades, his bosom pierced: its edge was famed with the Frisian earls.

On fierce-heart Finn there fell likewise, on himself at home, the horrid sword-death; for Guthlaf and Oslaf of grim attack had sorrowing told, from sea-ways landed, mourning their woes.[1]

---

1. That is, these two Danes, escaping home, had told the story of the attack on Hnaef, the slaying of Hengest, and all the Danish woes. Collecting a force, they return to Frisia and kill Finn in his home.

Finn's wavering spirit bode not in breast. The burg was reddened with blood of foemen, and Finn was slain, king amid clansmen; the queen was taken.

To their ship the Scylding warriors bore all the chattels the chieftain owned, whatever they found in Finn's domain of gems and jewels. The gentle wife o'er paths of the deep to the Danes they bore, led to her land.

The lay was finished, the gleeman's song. Then glad rose the revel; bench-joy brightened. Bearers draw from their "wonder-vats" wine.

Comes Wealhtheow forth, under gold-crown goes where the good pair sit, uncle and nephew, true each to the other one, kindred in amity. Unferth the spokesman at the Scylding lord's feet sat: men had faith in his spirit, his keenness of courage, though kinsmen had found him unsure at the sword-play.

The Scylding queen spoke: "Quaff of this cup, my king and lord, breaker of rings, and blithe be thou, gold-friend of men; to the Geats here speak such words of mildness as man should use. Be glad with thy Geats; of those gifts be mindful, or near or far, which now thou hast. Men say to me, as son thou wishest yon hero to hold. Thy Heorot purged, jewel-hall brightest, enjoy while thou canst, with many a largess; and leave to thy kin folk and realm when forth thou goest to greet thy doom.

For gracious I deem my Hrothulf,[2] willing to hold and rule nobly our youths, if thou yield up first, prince of Scyldings, thy part in the world.

---

2. Nephew to Hrothgar, with whom he subsequently quarrels, and elder cousin to the two young sons of Hrothgar and Wealhtheow,—their natural guardian in the event of the king's death. There is something finely feminine in this speech of Wealhtheow's, apart from its somewhat irregular and irrelevant sequence of topics. Both she and her lord probably distrust Hrothulf; but she bids the king to be of good cheer, and, turning to the

I ween with good he will well requite offspring of ours, when all he minds that for him we did in his helpless days of gift and grace to gain him honor!"

Then she turned to the seat where her sons were placed, Hrethric and Hrothmund, with heroes' bairns, young men together: the Geat, too, sat there, Beowulf brave, the brothers between.

---

suspect, heaps affectionate assurances on his probity. "My own Hrothulf" will surely not forget these favors and benefits of the past, but will repay them to the orphaned boy.

XVIII

A CUP she gave him, with kindly greeting and winsome words. Of wounden gold, she offered, to honor him, arm-jewels twain, corselet and rings, and of collars the noblest that ever I knew the earth around.

Ne'er heard I so mighty, 'neath heaven's dome, a hoard-gem of heroes, since Hama bore to his bright-built burg the Brisings' necklace, jewel and gem casket.—

Jealousy fled he, Eormenric's hate: chose help eternal. Hygelac Geat, grandson of Swerting, on the last of his raids this ring bore with him, under his banner the booty defending, the war-spoil warding; but Wyrd o'erwhelmed him what time, in his daring, dangers he sought, feud with Frisians.

Fairest of gems he bore with him over the beaker-of-waves, sovran strong: under shield he died.

Fell the corpse of the king into keeping of Franks, gear of the breast, and that gorgeous ring; weaker warriors won the spoil, after gripe of battle, from Geatland's lord, and held the death-field.

Din rose in hall. Wealhtheow spake amid warriors, and said:—

"This jewel enjoy in thy jocund youth, Beowulf lov'd, these battle-weeds wear, a royal treasure, and richly thrive! Preserve thy strength, and these striplings here counsel in kindness: requital be mine.

Hast done such deeds, that for days to come thou art famed among folk both far and near, so wide as washeth the wave of Ocean his windy walls. Through the ways of life prosper, O prince! I pray for thee rich possessions. To son of mine be helpful in deed and uphold his joys! Here every earl to the other is true, mild of mood, to the master loyal! Thanes are friendly, the throng obedient, liegemen are revelling: list and obey!"

Went then to her place.—That was proudest of feasts; flowed wine for the warriors. Wyrd they knew not, destiny dire, and the doom to be seen by many an earl when eve should come, and Hrothgar homeward hasten away, royal, to rest.

The room was guarded by an army of earls, as erst was done. They bared the bench-boards; abroad they spread beds and bolsters.—One beer-carouser in danger of doom lay down in the hall.—At their heads they set their shields of war, bucklers bright; on the bench were there over each atheling, easy to see, the high battle-helmet, the haughty spear, the corselet of rings.

'Twas their custom so ever to be for battle prepared, at home, or harrying, which it were, even as oft as evil threatened their sovran king.—They were clansmen good.

XIX

THEN sank they to sleep.

With sorrow one bought his rest of the evening,—as ofttime had happened when Grendel guarded that golden hall, evil wrought, till his end drew nigh, slaughter for sins.

'Twas seen and told how an avenger survived the fiend, as was learned afar.

The livelong time after that grim fight, Grendel's mother, monster of women, mourned her woe. She was doomed to dwell in the dreary waters, cold sea-courses, since Cain cut down with edge of the sword his only brother, his father's offspring: outlawed he fled, marked with murder, from men's delights warded the wilds.—

There woke from him such fate-sent ghosts as Grendel, who, war-wolf horrid, at Heorot found a warrior watching and waiting the fray, with whom the grisly one grappled amain.

But the man remembered his mighty power, the glorious gift that God had sent him, in his Maker's mercy put his trust for comfort and help: so he conquered the foe, felled the fiend, who fled abject, reft of joy, to the realms of death, mankind's foe.

And his mother now, gloomy and grim, would go that quest of sorrow, the death of her son to avenge.

To Heorot came she, where helmeted Danes slept in the hall. Too soon came back old ills of the earls, when in she burst, the mother of Grendel.

Less grim, though, that terror, e'en as terror of woman in war is less, might of maid, than of men in arms when, hammer-forged, the falchion hard, sword gore-stained, through swine of the helm, crested, with keen blade carves amain.

Then was in hall the hard-edge drawn, the swords on the settles,[1] and shields a-many firm held in hand: nor helmet minded nor harness of mail, whom that horror seized. Haste was hers; she would hie afar and save her life when the liegemen saw her.

Yet a single atheling up she seized fast and firm, as she fled to the moor. He was for Hrothgar of heroes the dearest, of trusty vassals betwixt the seas, whom she killed on his couch, a clansman famous, in battle brave.—Nor was Beowulf there; another house had been held apart, after giving of gold, for the Geat renowned.—

Uproar filled Heorot; the hand all had viewed, blood-flecked, she bore with her; bale was returned, dole in the dwellings: 'twas dire exchange where Dane and Geat were doomed to give the lives of loved ones.

Long-tried king, the hoary hero, at heart was sad when he knew his noble no more lived, and dead indeed was his dearest thane.

To his bower was Beowulf brought in haste, dauntless victor. As daylight broke, along with his earls the atheling lord, with his clansmen, came where the king abode waiting to see if the Wielder-of-All would turn this tale of trouble and woe.

1. They had laid their arms on the benches near where they slept.

Strode o'er floor the famed-in-strife, with his hand-companions,—the hall resounded,—wishing to greet the wise old king, Ingwines' lord; he asked if the night had passed in peace to the prince's mind.

XX

HROTHGAR spake, helmet-of-Scyldings:—

"Ask not of pleasure! Pain is renewed to Danish folk.

Dead is Aeschere, of Yrmenlaf the elder brother, my sage adviser and stay in council, shoulder-comrade in stress of fight when warriors clashed and we warded our heads, hewed the helm-boars; hero famed should be every earl as Aeschere was!

But here in Heorot a hand hath slain him of wandering death-sprite. I wot not whither,[1] proud of the prey, her path she took, fain of her fill.

The feud she avenged that yesternight, unyieldingly, Grendel in grimmest grasp thou killedst,—seeing how long these liegemen mine he ruined and ravaged. Reft of life, in arms he fell.

Now another comes, keen and cruel, her kin to avenge, faring far in feud of blood: so that many a thane shall think, who e'er sorrows in soul for that sharer of rings, this is hardest of heart-bales.

The hand lies low that once was willing each wish to please.

---

1. He surmises presently where she is.

Land-dwellers here[2] and liegemen mine, who house by those parts, I have heard relate that such a pair they have sometimes seen, march-stalkers mighty the moorland haunting, wandering spirits: one of them seemed, so far as my folk could fairly judge, of womankind; and one, accursed, in man's guise trod the misery-track of exile, though huger than human bulk.

Grendel in days long gone they named him, folk of the land; his father they knew not, nor any brood that was born to him of treacherous spirits.

Untrod is their home; by wolf-cliffs haunt they and windy headlands, fenways fearful, where flows the stream from mountains gliding to gloom of the rocks, underground flood.

Not far is it hence in measure of miles that the mere expands, and o'er it the frost-bound forest hanging, sturdily rooted, shadows the wave.

By night is a wonder weird to see, fire on the waters. So wise lived none of the sons of men, to search those depths!

Nay, though the heath-rover, harried by dogs, the horn-proud hart, this holt should seek, long distance driven, his dear life first on the brink he yields ere he brave the plunge to hide his head: 'tis no happy place!

Thence the welter of waters washes up wan to welkin when winds bestir evil storms, and air grows dusk, and the heavens weep.

---

2. The connection is not difficult. The words of mourning, of acute grief, are said; and according to Germanic sequence of thought, inexorable here, the next and only topic is revenge. But is it possible? Hrothgar leads up to his appeal and promise with a skillful and often effective description of the horrors which surround the monster's home and await the attempt of an avenging foe.

Now is help once more with thee alone!

The land thou knowst not, place of fear, where thou findest out that sin-flecked being. Seek if thou dare! I will reward thee, for waging this fight, with ancient treasure, as erst I did, with winding gold, if thou winnest back."

XXI

BEOWULF spake, bairn of Ecgtheow:

"Sorrow not, sage! It beseems us better friends to avenge than fruitlessly mourn them.

Each of us all must his end abide in the ways of the world; so win who may glory ere death! When his days are told, that is the warrior's worthiest doom.

Rise, O realm-warder! Ride we anon, and mark the trail of the mother of Grendel. No harbor shall hide her—heed my promise!—enfolding of field or forested mountain or floor of the flood, let her flee where she will! But thou this day endure in patience, as I ween thou wilt, thy woes each one."

Leaped up the graybeard: God he thanked, mighty Lord, for the man's brave words.

For Hrothgar soon a horse was saddled wave-maned steed. The sovran wise stately rode on; his shield-armed men followed in force.

The footprints led along the woodland, widely seen, a path o'er the plain, where she passed, and trod the murky moor; of men-at-arms she bore the bravest and best one, dead, him who with Hrothgar the homestead ruled.

On then went the atheling-born o'er stone-cliffs steep and strait defiles, narrow passes and unknown ways, headlands sheer, and the haunts of the Nicors.

Foremost he[1] fared, a few at his side of the wiser men, the ways to scan, till he found in a flash the forested hill hanging over the hoary rock, a woful wood: the waves below were dyed in blood.

The Danish men had sorrow of soul, and for Scyldings all, for many a hero, 'twas hard to bear, ill for earls, when Aeschere's head they found by the flood on the foreland there.

Waves were welling, the warriors saw, hot with blood; but the horn sang oft battle-song bold.

The band sat down, and watched on the water worm-like things, sea-dragons strange that sounded the deep, and nicors that lay on the ledge of the ness—such as oft essay at hour of morn on the road-of-sails their ruthless quest,—and sea-snakes and monsters. These started away, swollen and savage that song to hear, that war-horn's blast.

The warden of Geats, with bolt from bow, then balked of life, of wave-work, one monster, amid its heart went the keen war-shaft; in water it seemed less doughty in swimming whom death had seized.

Swift on the billows, with boar-spears well hooked and barbed, it was hard beset, done to death and dragged on the headland, wave-roamer wondrous. Warriors viewed the grisly guest.

Then girt him Beowulf in martial mail, nor mourned for his life. His breastplate broad and bright of hues, woven by hand, should the waters try; well could it ward the warrior's body that battle should break on his breast in vain nor harm his heart by the hand of a foe. And the helmet

1. Hrothgar is probably meant.

white that his head protected was destined to dare the deeps of the flood, through wave-whirl win: 'twas wound with chains, decked with gold, as in days of yore the weapon-smith worked it wondrously, with swine-forms set it, that swords nowise, brandished in battle, could bite that helm.

Nor was that the meanest of mighty helps which Hrothgar's orator offered at need: "Hrunting" they named the hilted sword, of old-time heirlooms easily first; iron was its edge, all etched with poison, with battle-blood hardened, nor blenched it at fight in hero's hand who held it ever, on paths of peril prepared to go to folkstead[2] of foes.

Not first time this it was destined to do a daring task. For he bore not in mind, the bairn of Ecglaf sturdy and strong, that speech he had made, drunk with wine, now this weapon he lent to a stouter swordsman.

Himself, though, durst not under welter of waters wager his life as loyal liegeman. So lost he his glory, honor of earls. With the other not so, who girded him now for the grim encounter.

---

2. Meeting place.

XXI

BEOWULF spake, bairn of Ecgtheow:—

"Have mind, thou honored offspring of Healfdene gold-friend of men, now I go on this quest, sovran wise, what once was said: if in thy cause it came that I should lose my life, thou wouldst loyal bide to me, though fallen, in father's place!

Be guardian, thou, to this group of my thanes, my warrior-friends, if War should seize me; and the goodly gifts thou gavest me, Hrothgar beloved, to Hygelac send!

Geatland's king may ken by the gold, Hrethel's son see, when he stares at the treasure, that I got me a friend for goodness famed, and joyed while I could in my jewel-bestower.

And let Unferth wield this wondrous sword, earl far-honored, this heirloom precious, hard of edge: with Hrunting I seek doom of glory, or Death shall take me."

After these words the Weder-Geat lord boldly hastened, biding never answer at all: the ocean floods closed o'er the hero. Long while of the day fled ere he felt the floor of the sea.

Soon found the fiend who the flood-domain sword-hungry held these hundred winters, greedy and grim, that some guest from above, some man, was raiding her monster-realm.

She grasped out for him with grisly claws, and the warrior seized; yet scathed she not his body hale; the breastplate hindered, as she strove to shatter the sark of war, the linked harness, with loathsome hand.

Then bore this brine-wolf, when bottom she touched, the lord of rings to the lair she haunted whiles vainly he strove, though his valor held, weapon to wield against wondrous monsters that sore beset him; sea-beasts many tried with fierce tusks to tear his mail, and swarmed on the stranger.

But soon he marked he was now in some hall, he knew not which, where water never could work him harm, nor through the roof could reach him ever fangs of the flood.

Firelight he saw, beams of a blaze that brightly shone.

Then the warrior was ware of that wolf-of-the-deep, mere-wife monstrous. For mighty stroke he swung his blade, and the blow withheld not.

Then sang on her head that seemly blade its war-song wild.

But the warrior found the light-of-battle[1] was loath to bite, to harm the heart: its hard edge failed the noble at need, yet had known of old strife hand to hand, and had helmets cloven, doomed men's fighting-gear. First time, this, for the gleaming blade that its glory fell.

Firm still stood, nor failed in valor, heedful of high deeds, Hygelac's kinsman; flung away fretted sword, featly jewelled, the angry earl; on earth it lay steel-edged and stiff.

1. Kenning for "sword." Hrunting is bewitched, laid under a spell of uselessness, along with all other swords.

His strength he trusted, hand-gripe of might. So man shall do whenever in war he weens to earn him lasting fame, nor fears for his life!

Seized then by shoulder, shrank not from combat, the Geatish war-prince Grendel's mother. Flung then the fierce one, filled with wrath, his deadly foe, that she fell to ground.

Swift on her part she paid him back with grisly grasp, and grappled with him. Spent with struggle, stumbled the warrior, fiercest of fighting-men, fell adown.

On the hall-guest she hurled herself, hent her short sword, broad and brown-edged,[2] the bairn to avenge, the sole-born son.—On his shoulder lay braided breast-mail, barring death, withstanding entrance of edge or blade.

Life would have ended for Ecgtheow's son, under wide earth for that earl of Geats, had his armor of war not aided him, battle-net hard, and holy God wielded the victory, wisest Maker.

The Lord of Heaven allowed his cause; and easily rose the earl erect.

---

2. This brown of swords, evidently meaning burnished, bright, continues to be a favorite adjective in the popular ballads.

XXIII

'MID the battle-gear saw he a blade triumphant, old-sword of Eotens, with edge of proof, warriors' heirloom, weapon unmatched,—save only 'twas more than other men to bandy-of-battle could bear at all—as the giants had wrought it, ready and keen.

Seized then its chain-hilt the Scyldings' chieftain, bold and battle-grim, brandished the sword, reckless of life, and so wrathfully smote that it gripped her neck and grasped her hard, her bone-rings breaking: the blade pierced through that fated-one's flesh: to floor she sank.

Bloody the blade: he was blithe of his deed.

Then blazed forth light. 'Twas bright within as when from the sky there shines unclouded heaven's candle. The hall he scanned.

By the wall then went he; his weapon raised high by its hilts the Hygelac-thane, angry and eager. That edge was not useless to the warrior now.

He wished with speed Grendel to guerdon for grim raids many, for the war he waged on Western-Danes oftener far than an only time, when of Hrothgar's hearth-companions he slew in slumber, in sleep devoured, fifteen men of the folk of Danes, and as many others outward bore, his horrible prey.

Well paid for that the wrathful prince! For now prone he saw Grendel stretched there, spent with war, spoiled of life, so scathed had left him Heorot's battle.

The body sprang far when after death it endured the blow, sword-stroke savage, that severed its head.

Soon,[1] then, saw the sage companions who waited with Hrothgar, watching the flood, that the tossing waters turbid grew, blood-stained the mere.

Old men together, hoary-haired, of the hero spake; the warrior would not, they weened, again, proud of conquest, come to seek their mighty master. To many it seemed the wolf-of-the-waves had won his life.

The ninth hour came. The noble Scyldings left the headland; homeward went the gold-friend of men.[2] But the guests sat on, stared at the surges, sick in heart, and wished, yet weened not, their winsome lord again to see.

Now that sword began, from blood of the fight, in battle-droppings,[3] war-blade, to wane: 'twas a wondrous thing that all of it melted as ice is wont when frosty fetters the Father loosens, unwinds the wave-bonds, wielding all seasons and times: the true God he!

Nor took from that dwelling the duke of the Geats save only the head and that hilt withal blazoned with jewels: the blade had melted, burned was the bright sword, her blood was so hot, so poisoned the hell-sprite who perished within there.

Soon he was swimming who safe saw in combat downfall of demons; up-dove through the flood. The clashing

1. After the killing of the monster and Grendel's decapitation.
2. Hrothgar.
3. The blade slowly dissolves in blood-stained drops like icicles.

waters were cleansed now, waste of waves, where the wandering fiend her life-days left and this lapsing world.

Swam then to strand the sailors'-refuge, sturdy-in-spirit, of sea-booty glad, of burden brave he bore with him.

Went then to greet him, and God they thanked, the thane-band choice of their chieftain blithe, that safe and sound they could see him again.

Soon from the hardy one helmet and armor deftly they doffed: now drowsed the mere, water 'neath welkin, with war-blood stained.

Forth they fared by the footpaths thence, merry at heart the highways measured, well-known roads.

Courageous men carried the head from the cliff by the sea, an arduous task for all the band, the firm in fight, since four were needed on the shaft-of-slaughter[4] strenuously to bear to the gold-hall Grendel's head.

So presently to the palace there foemen fearless, fourteen Geats, marching came. Their master-of-clan mighty amid them the meadow-ways trod. Strode then within the sovran thane fearless in fight, of fame renowned, hardy hero, Hrothgar to greet.

And next by the hair into hall was borne Grendel's head, where the henchmen were drinking, an awe to clan and queen alike, a monster of marvel: the men looked on.

---

4. Spear.

XXIV

BEOWULF spake, bairn of Ecgtheow:—

"Lo, now, this sea-booty, son of Healfdene, Lord of Scyldings, we've lustily brought thee, sign of glory; thou seest it here.

Not lightly did I with my life escape!

In war under water this work I essayed with endless effort; and even so my strength had been lost had the Lord not shielded me.

Not a whit could I with Hrunting do in work of war, though the weapon is good; yet a sword the Sovran of Men vouchsafed me to spy on the wall there, in splendor hanging, old, gigantic,—how oft He guides the friendless wight!—and I fought with that brand, felling in fight, since fate was with me, the house's wardens.

That war-sword then all burned, bright blade, when the blood gushed o'er it, battle-sweat hot; but the hilt I brought back from my foes.

So avenged I their fiendish deeds death-fall of Danes, as was due and right. And this is my hest, that in Heorot now safe thou canst sleep with thy soldier band, and every thane of all thy folk both old and young; no evil fear, Scyldings' lord, from that side again, aught ill for thy earls, as erst thou must!"

Then the golden hilt, for that gray-haired leader, hoary hero, in hand was laid, giant-wrought, old. So owned and enjoyed it after downfall of devils, the Danish lord, wonder-smiths' work, since the world was rid of that grim-souled fiend, the foe of God, murder-marked, and his mother as well.

Now it passed into power of the people's king, best of all that the oceans bound who have scattered their gold o'er Scandia's isle.

Hrothgar spake—the hilt he viewed, heirloom old, where was etched the rise of that far-off fight when the floods o'erwhelmed, raging waves, the race of giants (fearful their fate!), a folk estranged from God Eternal: whence guerdon due in that waste of waters the Wielder paid them.

So on the guard of shining gold in runic staves it was rightly said for whom the serpent-traced sword was wrought, best of blades, in bygone days, and the hilt well wound.—The wise-one spake, son of Healfdene; silent were all:—

"Lo, so may he say who sooth and right follows 'mid folk, of far times mindful, a land-warden old,[1] that this earl belongs to the better breed!

So, borne aloft, thy fame must fly, O friend my Beowulf, far and wide o'er folksteads many. Firmly thou shalt all maintain, mighty strength with mood of wisdom. Love of mine will I assure thee, as, awhile ago, I promised; thou shalt prove a stay in future, in far-off years, to folk of thine, to the heroes a help.

Was not Heremod thus to offspring of Ecgwela, Honor-Scyldings, nor grew for their grace, but for grisly slaughter, for doom of death to the Danishmen.

---

1. That is, "whoever has as wide authority as I have and can remember so far back so many instances of heroism, may well say, as I say, that no better hero ever lived than Beowulf."

He slew, wrath-swollen, his shoulder-comrades, companions at board! So he passed alone, chieftain haughty, from human cheer. Though him the Maker with might endowed, delights of power, and uplifted high above all men, yet blood-fierce his mind, his breast-hoard, grew, no bracelets gave he to Danes as was due; he endured all joyless strain of struggle and stress of woe, long feud with his folk.

Here find thy lesson! Of virtue advise thee! This verse I have said for thee, wise from lapsed winters.

Wondrous seems how to sons of men Almighty God in the strength of His spirit sendeth wisdom, estate, high station: He swayeth all things. Whiles He letteth right lustily fare the heart of the hero of high-born race,—in seat ancestral assigns him bliss, his folk's sure fortress in fee to hold, puts in his power great parts of the earth, empire so ample, that end of it this wanter-of-wisdom weeneth none.

So he waxes in wealth, nowise can harm him illness or age; no evil cares shadow his spirit; no sword-hate threatens from ever an enemy: all the world wends at his will, no worse he knoweth, till all within him obstinate pride waxes and wakes while the warden slumbers, the spirit's sentry; sleep is too fast which masters his might, and the murderer nears, stealthily shooting the shafts from his bow!

XXV

"UNDER harness his heart then is hit indeed by sharpest shafts; and no shelter avails from foul behest of the hellish fiend.[1]

Him seems too little what long he possessed. Greedy and grim, no golden rings he gives for his pride; the promised future forgets he and spurns, with all God has sent him, Wonder-Wielder, of wealth and fame.

Yet in the end it ever comes that the frame of the body fragile yields, fated falls; and there follows another who joyously the jewels divides, the royal riches, nor recks of his forebear.

Ban, then, such baleful thoughts, Beowulf dearest, best of men, and the better part choose, profit eternal; and temper thy pride, warrior famous!

The flower of thy might lasts now a while: but erelong it shall be that sickness or sword thy strength shall minish, or fang of fire, or flooding billow, or bite of blade, or brandished spear, or odious age; or the eyes' clear beam wax dull and darken: Death even thee in haste shall o'erwhelm, thou hero of war!

So the Ring-Danes these half-years a hundred I ruled, wielded 'neath welkin, and warded them bravely from

---

1. That is, he is now undefended by conscience from the temptations (shafts) of the devil.

mighty-ones many o'er middle-earth, from spear and sword, till it seemed for me no foe could be found under fold of the sky. Lo, sudden the shift!

To me seated secure came grief for joy when Grendel began to harry my home, the hellish foe; for those ruthless raids, unresting I suffered heart-sorrow heavy.

Heaven be thanked, Lord Eternal, for life extended that I on this head all hewn and bloody, after long evil, with eyes may gaze!—Go to the bench now! Be glad at banquet, warrior worthy! A wealth of treasure at dawn of day, be dealt between us!"

Glad was the Geats' lord, going betimes to seek his seat, as the Sage commanded.

Afresh, as before, for the famed-in-battle, for the band of the hall, was a banquet dight nobly anew. The Night-Helm darkened dusk o'er the drinkers. The doughty ones rose: for the hoary-headed would hasten to rest, aged Scylding; and eager the Geat, shield-fighter sturdy, for sleeping yearned. Him wander-weary, warrior-guest from far, a hall-thane heralded forth, who by custom courtly cared for all needs of a thane as in those old days warrior-wanderers wont to have.

So slumbered the stout-heart.

Stately the hall rose gabled and gilt where the guest slept on till a raven black the rapture-of-heaven[2] blithe-heart boded. Bright came flying shine after shadow.

The swordsmen hastened, athelings all were eager homeward forth to fare; and far from thence the great-hearted guest would guide his keel.

---

2. Kenning for the sun.— This is a strange role for the raven. He is the warrior's bird of battle, exults in slaughter and carnage; his joy here is a compliment to the sunrise.

Bade then the hardy-one Hrunting be brought to the son of Ecglaf, the sword bade him take, excellent iron, and uttered his thanks for it, quoth that he counted it keen in battle, "war-friend" winsome: with words he slandered not edge of the blade: 'twas a big-hearted man!

Now eager for parting and armed at point warriors waited, while went to his host that Darling of Danes. The doughty atheling to high-seat hastened and Hrothgar greeted.

XXVI

BEOWULF spake, bairn of Ecgtheow:—

"Lo, we seafarers say our will, far-come men, that we fain would seek Hygelac now.

We here have found hosts to our heart: thou hast harbored us well. If ever on earth I am able to win me more of thy love, O lord of men, aught anew, than I now have done, for work of war I am willing still!

If it come to me ever across the seas that neighbor foemen annoy and fright thee,—as they that hate thee erewhile have used,—thousands then of thanes I shall bring, heroes to help thee.

Of Hygelac I know, ward of his folk, that, though few his years, the lord of the Geats will give me aid by word and by work, that well I may serve thee, wielding the war-wood to win thy triumph and lending thee might when thou lackest men.

If thy Hrethric should come to court of Geats, a sovran's son, he will surely there find his friends. A far-off land each man should visit who vaunts him brave."

Him then answering, Hrothgar spake:—

"These words of thine the wisest God sent to thy soul!

No sager counsel from so young in years e'er yet have I heard. Thou art strong of main and in mind art wary, art wise in words!

I ween indeed if ever it hap that Hrethel's heir by spear be seized, by sword-grim battle, by illness or iron, thine elder and lord, people's leader,—and life be thine,—no seemlier man will the Sea-Geats find at all to choose for their chief and king, for hoard-guard of heroes, if hold thou wilt thy kinsman's kingdom!

Thy keen mind pleases me the longer the better, Beowulf loved! Thou hast brought it about that both our peoples, sons of the Geat and Spear-Dane folk, shall have mutual peace, and from murderous strife, such as once they waged, from war refrain.

Long as I rule this realm so wide, let our hoards be common, let heroes with gold each other greet o'er the gannet's-bath, and the ringed-prow bear o'er rolling waves tokens of love. I trow my landfolk towards friend and foe are firmly joined, and honor they keep in the olden way."

To him in the hall, then, Healfdene's son gave treasures twelve, and the trust-of-earls bade him fare with the gifts to his folk beloved, hale to his home, and in haste return.

Then kissed the king of kin renowned, Scyldings' chieftain, that choicest thane, and fell on his neck.

Fast flowed the tears of the hoary-headed. Heavy with winters, he had chances twain, but he clung to this,[1]—that each should look on the other again, and hear him in hall. Was this hero so dear to him. his breast's wild billows he banned in vain; safe in his soul a secret longing, locked in his mind, for that loved man burned in his blood.

---

1. That is, he might or might not see Beowulf again. Old as he was, the latter chance was likely; but he clung to the former, hoping to see his young friend again "and exchange brave words in the hall."

Then Beowulf strode, glad of his gold-gifts, the grass-plot o'er, warrior blithe. The wave-roamer bode riding at anchor, its owner awaiting.

As they hastened onward, Hrothgar's gift they lauded at length.—'Twas a lord unpeered, every way blameless, till age had broken—it spareth no mortal—his splendid might.

XXVII

CAME now to ocean the ever-courageous hardy henchmen, their harness bearing, woven war-sarks.

The warden marked, trusty as ever, the earl's return. From the height of the hill no hostile words reached the guests as he rode to greet them; but "Welcome!" he called to that Weder clan as the sheen-mailed spoilers to ship marched on.

Then on the strand, with steeds and treasure and armor their roomy and ring-dight ship was heavily laden: high its mast rose over Hrothgar's hoarded gems.

A sword to the boat-guard Beowulf gave, mounted with gold; on the mead-bench since he was better esteemed, that blade possessing, heirloom old.

—Their ocean-keel boarding, they drove through the deep, and Daneland left.

A sea-cloth was set, a sail with ropes, firm to the mast; the flood-timbers moaned;[1] nor did wind over billows that wave-swimmer blow across from her course. The craft sped on, foam-necked it floated forth o'er the waves, keel firm-bound over briny currents, till they got them sight of the Geatish cliffs, home-known headlands.

High the boat, stirred by winds, on the strand updrove.

1. With the speed of the boat.

Helpful at haven the harbor-guard stood, who long already for loved companions by the water had waited and watched afar. He bound to the beach the broad-bosomed ship with anchor-bands, lest ocean-billows that trusty timber should tear away.

Then Beowulf bade them bear the treasure, gold and jewels; no journey far was it thence to go to the giver of rings, Hygelac Hrethling: at home he dwelt by the sea-wall close, himself and clan.

Haughty that house, a hero the king, high the hall, and Hygd[2] right young, wise and wary, though winters few in those fortress walls she had found a home, Haereth's daughter.

Nor humble her ways, nor grudged she gifts to the Geatish men, of precious treasure. Not Thryth's pride showed she, folk-queen famed, or that fell deceit.

Was none so daring that durst make bold (save her lord alone) of the liegemen dear that lady full in the face to look, but forged fetters he found his lot, bonds of death!

And brief the respite; soon as they seized him, his sword-doom was spoken, and the burnished blade a baleful murder proclaimed and closed.

No queenly way for woman to practise, though peerless she, that the weaver-of-peace[3] from warrior dear by wrath and lying his life should reave!

But Hemming's kinsman hindered this.—For over their ale men also told that of these folk-horrors fewer she wrought, onslaughts of evil, after she went, gold-decked bride, to the brave young prince, atheling haughty, and

---

2. Queen to Hygelac. She is praised by contrast with the antitype, Thryth, just as Beowulf was praised by contrast with Heremod.

3. Kenning for "wife."

Offa's hall o'er the fallow flood at her father's bidding safely sought, where since she prospered, royal, throned, rich in goods, fain of the fair life fate had sent her, and leal in love to the lord of warriors.

He, of all heroes I heard of ever from sea to sea, of the sons of earth, most excellent seemed.

Hence Offa was praised for his fighting and feeing by far-off men, the spear-bold warrior; wisely he ruled over his empire. Eomer woke to him, help of heroes, Hemming's kinsman, Grandson of Garmund, grim in war.

XXVIII

HASTENED the hardy one, henchmen with him, sandy strand of the sea to tread and widespread ways. The world's great candle, sun shone from south.

They strode along with sturdy steps to the spot they knew where the battle-king young, his burg within, slayer of Ongentheow, shared the rings, shelter-of-heroes.

To Hygelac Beowulf's coming was quickly told,—that there in the court the clansmen's refuge, the shield-companion sound and alive, hale from the hero-play homeward strode.

With haste in the hall, by highest order, room for the rovers was readily made. By his sovran he sat, come safe from battle, kinsman by kinsman.

His kindly lord he first had greeted in gracious form, with manly words.

The mead dispensing, came through the high hall Haereth's daughter, winsome to warriors, wine-cup bore to the hands of the heroes.

Hygelac then his comrade fairly with question plied in the lofty hall, sore longing to know what manner of sojourn the Sea-Geats made. "What came of thy quest, my kinsman Beowulf, when thy yearnings suddenly swept thee yonder battle to seek o'er the briny sea, combat in Heorot? Hrothgar couldst thou aid at all, the honored chief, in his wide-known woes? With waves of care my sad heart seethed; I sore mistrusted my loved one's venture: long I begged thee by no means to seek that slaughtering monster, but suffer the South-Danes to settle their feud themselves with Grendel. Now God be thanked that safe and sound I can see thee now!"

Beowulf spake, the bairn of Ecgtheow:—

"'Tis known and unhidden, Hygelac Lord, to many men, that meeting of ours, struggle grim between Grendel and me, which we fought on the field where full too many sorrows he wrought for the Scylding-Victors, evils unending.

These all I avenged.

No boast can be from breed of Grendel, any on earth, for that uproar at dawn, from the longest-lived of the loathsome race in fleshly fold!—

But first I went Hrothgar to greet in the hall of gifts, where Healfdene's kinsman high-renowned, soon as my purpose was plain to him, assigned me a seat by his son and heir.

The liegemen were lusty; my life-days never such merry men over mead in hall have I heard under heaven!

The high-born queen, people's peace-bringer, passed through the hall, cheered the young clansmen, clasps of gold, ere she sought her seat, to sundry gave. Oft to the heroes Hrothgar's daughter, to earls in turn, the ale-cup tendered,—she whom I heard these hall-companions Freawaru name, when fretted gold she proffered the warriors.

Promised is she, gold-decked maid, to the glad son of Froda. Sage this seems to the Scylding's-friend, kingdom's-keeper: he counts it wise the woman to wed so and ward off feud, store of slaughter.

But seldom ever when men are slain, does the murder-spear sink but briefest while, though the bride be fair![1]

"Nor haply will like it the Heathobard lord, and as little each of his liegemen all, when a thane of the Danes, in that doughty throng, goes with the lady along their hall, and on him the old-time heirlooms glisten hard and ring-decked, Heathobard's treasure, weapons that once they wielded fair until they lost at the linden-play[2] liegeman leal and their lives as well.

Then, over the ale, on this heirloom gazing, some ash-wielder old who has all in mind that spear-death of men,[3]—he is stern of mood, heavy at heart,—in the hero young tests the temper and tries the soul and war-hate wakens, with words like these:—

Canst thou not, comrade, ken that sword which to the fray thy father carried in his final feud, 'neath the fighting-mask, dearest of blades, when the Danish slew him and

---

1. Beowulf gives his uncle the king not mere gossip of his journey, but a statesmanlike forecast of the outcome of certain policies at the Danish court. Talk of interpolation here is absurd. As both Beowulf and Hygelac know,—and the folk for whom the Beowulf was put together also knew,—Froda was king of the Heathobards (probably the Langobards, once near neighbors of Angle and Saxon tribes on the continent), and had fallen in fight with the Danes. Hrothgar will set aside this feud by giving his daughter as "peace-weaver" and wife to the young king Ingeld, son of the slain Froda. But Beowulf, on general principles and from his observation of the particular case, foretells trouble.

2. Play of shields, battle. A Danish warrior cuts down Froda in the fight, and takes his sword and armor, leaving them to a son. This son is selected to accompany his mistress, the young princess Freawaru, to her new home when she is Ingeld's queen. Heedlessly he wears the sword of Froda in hall. An old warrior points it out to Ingeld, and eggs him on to vengeance. At his instigation the Dane is killed; but the murderer, afraid of results, and knowing the land, escapes. So the old feud must break out again.

3. That is, their disastrous battle and the slaying of their king.

wielded the war-place on Withergild's fall, after havoc of heroes, those hardy Scyldings? Now, the son of a certain slaughtering Dane, proud of his treasure, paces this hall, joys in the killing, and carries the jewel[4] that rightfully ought to be owned by thee!

Thus he urges and eggs him all the time with keenest words, till occasion offers that Freawaru's thane, for his father's deed, after bite of brand in his blood must slumber, losing his life; but that liegeman flies living away, for the land he kens.

And thus be broken on both their sides oaths of the earls, when Ingeld's breast wells with war-hate, and wife-love now after the care-billows cooler grows.

"So[5] I hold not high the Heathobards' faith due to the Danes, or their during love and pact of peace.—But I pass from that, turning to Grendel, O giver-of-treasure, and saying in full how the fight resulted, hand-fray of heroes.

When heaven's jewel had fled o'er far fields, that fierce sprite came, night-foe savage, to seek us out where safe and sound we sentried the hall.

To Hondscio then was that harassing deadly, his fall there was fated.

He first was slain, girded warrior. Grendel on him turned murderous mouth, on our mighty kinsman, and all of the brave man's body devoured.

Yet none the earlier, empty-handed, would the bloody-toothed murderer, mindful of bale, outward go from the

---

4. The sword.

5. Beowulf returns to his forecast. Things might well go somewhat as follows, he says; sketches a little tragic story; and with this prophecy by illustration returns to the tale of his adventure.

gold-decked hall: but me he attacked in his terror of might, with greedy hand grasped me.

A glove hung by him[6] wide and wondrous, wound with bands; and in artful wise it all was wrought, by devilish craft, of dragon-skins.

Me therein, an innocent man, the fiendish foe was fain to thrust with many another. He might not so, when I all angrily upright stood.

'Twere long to relate how that land-destroyer I paid in kind for his cruel deeds; yet there, my prince, this people of thine got fame by my fighting.

He fled away, and a little space his life preserved; but there staid behind him his stronger hand left in Heorot; heartsick thence on the floor of the ocean that outcast fell.

Me for this struggle the Scyldings'-friend paid in plenty with plates of gold, with many a treasure, when morn had come and we all at the banquet-board sat down.

Then was song and glee. The gray-haired Scylding, much tested, told of the times of yore. Whiles the hero his harp bestirred, wood-of-delight; now lays he chanted of sooth and sadness, or said aright legends of wonder, the wide-hearted king; or for years of his youth he would yearn at times, for strength of old struggles, now stricken with age, hoary hero: his heart surged full when, wise with winters, he wailed their flight.

Thus in the hall the whole of that day at ease we feasted, till fell o'er earth another night.

Anon full ready in greed of vengeance, Grendel's mother set forth all doleful.

---

6. Not an actual glove, but a sort of bag.

Dead was her son through war-hate of Weders; now, woman monstrous with fury fell a foeman she slew, avenged her offspring.

From Aeschere old, loyal councillor, life was gone; nor might they e'en, when morning broke, those Danish people, their death-done comrade burn with brands, on balefire lay the man they mourned.

Under mountain stream she had carried the corpse with cruel hands. For Hrothgar that was the heaviest sorrow of all that had laden the lord of his folk.

The leader then, by thy life, besought me (sad was his soul) in the sea-waves' coil to play the hero and hazard my being for glory of prowess: my guerdon he pledged.

I then in the waters—'tis widely known—that sea-floor-guardian savage found. Hand-to-hand there a while we struggled; billows welled blood; in the briny hall her head I hewed with a hardy blade from Grendel's mother,—and gained my life, though not without danger. My doom was not yet.

Then the haven-of-heroes, Healfdene's son, gave me in guerdon great gifts of price.

XXXI

"So held this king to the customs old, that I wanted for nought in the wage I gained, the meed of my might; he made me gifts, Healfdene's heir, for my own disposal.

Now to thee, my prince, I proffer them all, gladly give them. Thy grace alone can find me favor. Few indeed have I of kinsmen, save, Hygelac, thee!"

Then he bade them bear him the boar-head standard, the battle-helm high, and breastplate gray, the splendid sword; then spake in form:—

"Me this war-gear the wise old prince, Hrothgar, gave, and his hest he added, that its story be straightway said to thee.—

A while it was held by Heorogar king, for long time lord of the land of Scyldings; yet not to his son the sovran left it, to daring Heoroweard,—dear as he was to him, his harness of battle.—Well hold thou it all!"

And I heard that soon passed o'er the path of this treasure, all apple-fallow, four good steeds, each like the others, arms and horses he gave to the king. So should kinsmen be, not weave one another the net of wiles, or with deep-hid treachery death contrive for neighbor and comrade.

His nephew was ever by hardy Hygelac held full dear, and each kept watch o'er the other's weal.

I heard, too, the necklace to Hygd he presented, wonder-wrought treasure, which Wealhtheow gave him sovran's daughter: three steeds he added, slender and saddle-gay.

Since such gift the gem gleamed bright on the breast of the queen. Thus showed his strain the son of Ecgtheow as a man remarked for mighty deeds and acts of honor.

At ale he slew not comrade or kin; nor cruel his mood, though of sons of earth his strength was greatest, a glorious gift that God had sent the splendid leader.

Long was he spurned, and worthless by Geatish warriors held; him at mead the master-of-clans failed full oft to favor at all. Slack and shiftless the strong men deemed him, profitless prince; but payment came, to the warrior honored, for all his woes.—

Then the bulwark-of-earls[1] bade bring within, hardy chieftain, Hrethel's heirloom garnished with gold: no Geat e'er knew in shape of a sword a statelier prize.

The brand he laid in Beowulf's lap; and of hides assigned him seven thousand,[2] with house and high-seat. They held in common land alike by their line of birth, inheritance, home: but higher the king because of his rule o'er the realm itself.

Now further it fell with the flight of years, with harryings horrid, that Hygelac perished,[3] and Heardred, too, by hewing of swords under the shield-wall slaughtered lay,

---

1. Hygelac.

2. This is generally assumed to mean hides, though the text simply says "seven thousand." A hide in England meant about 120 acres, though "the size of the acre varied."

3. On the historical raid into Frankish territory between 512 and 520 a.d. The subsequent course of events, as gathered from hints of this epic, is partly told in Scandinavian legend.

when him at the van of his victor-folk sought hardy heroes, Heatho-Scilfings, in arms o'erwhelming Hereric's nephew.

Then Beowulf came as king this broad realm to wield; and he ruled it well fifty winters,[4] a wise old prince, warding his land, until One began in the dark of night, a Dragon, to rage.

In the grave on the hill a hoard it guarded, in the stone-barrow steep. A strait path reached it, unknown to mortals.

Some man, however, came by chance that cave within to the heathen hoard.[5] In hand he took a golden goblet, nor gave he it back, stole with it away, while the watcher slept, by thievish wiles: for the warden's wrath prince and people must pay betimes!

---

4. The chronology of this epic, as scholars have worked it out, would make Beowulf well over ninety years of age when he fights the dragon. But the fifty years of his reign need not be taken as historical fact.

5. The text is here hopelessly illegible, and only the general drift of the meaning can be rescued. For one thing, we have the old myth of a dragon who guards hidden treasure. But with this runs the story of some noble, last of his race, who hides all his wealth within this barrow and there chants his farewell to life's glories. After his death the dragon takes possession of the hoard and watches over it. A condemned or banished man, desperate, hides in the barrow, discovers the treasure, and while the dragon sleeps, makes off with a golden beaker or the like, and carries it for propitiation to his master. The dragon discovers the loss and exacts fearful penalty from the people round about.

XXXII

THAT way he went with no will of his own, in danger of life, to the dragon's hoard, but for pressure of peril, some prince's thane.

He fled in fear the fatal scourge, seeking shelter, a sinful man, and entered in. At the awful sight tottered that guest, and terror seized him; yet the wretched fugitive rallied anon from fright and fear ere he fled away, and took the cup from that treasure-hoard.

Of such besides there was store enough, heirlooms old, the earth below, which some earl forgotten, in ancient years, left the last of his lofty race, heedfully there had hidden away, dearest treasure.

For death of yore had hurried all hence; and he alone left to live, the last of the clan, weeping his friends, yet wished to bide warding the treasure, his one delight, though brief his respite.

The barrow, new-ready, to strand and sea-waves stood anear, hard by the headland, hidden and closed; there laid within it his lordly heirlooms and heaped hoard of heavy gold that warden of rings.

Few words he spake: "Now hold thou, earth, since heroes may not, what earls have owned!

Lo, erst from thee brave men brought it!

But battle-death seized and cruel killing my clansmen all, robbed them of life and a liegeman's joys. None have I left to lift the sword, or to cleanse the carven cup of price, beaker bright.

My brave are gone. And the helmet hard, all haughty with gold, shall part from its plating.

Polishers sleep who could brighten and burnish the battle-mask; and those weeds of war that were wont to brave over bicker of shields the bite of steel rust with their bearer.

The ringed mail fares not far with famous chieftain, at side of hero!

No harp's delight, no glee-wood's gladness! No good hawk now flies through the hall! Nor horses fleet stamp in the burgstead!

Battle and death the flower of my race have reft away."

Mournful of mood, thus he moaned his woe, alone, for them all, and unblithe wept by day and by night, till death's fell wave o'erwhelmed his heart.

His hoard-of-bliss that old ill-doer open found, who, blazing at twilight the barrows haunteth, naked foe-dragon flying by night folded in fire: the folk of earth dread him sore. 'Tis his doom to seek hoard in the graves, and heathen gold to watch, many-wintered: nor wins he thereby!

Powerful this plague-of-the-people thus held the house of the hoard in earth three hundred winters; till One aroused wrath in his breast, to the ruler bearing that costly cup, and the king implored for bond of peace.

So the barrow was plundered, borne off was booty. His boon was granted that wretched man; and his ruler saw first time what was fashioned in far-off days.

When the dragon awoke, new woe was kindled.

O'er the stone he snuffed. The stark-heart found foot-print of foe who so far had gone in his hidden craft by the creature's head.—So may the undoomed easily flee evils and exile, if only he gain the grace of The Wielder!

—That warden of gold o'er the ground went seeking, greedy to find the man who wrought him such wrong in sleep. Savage and burning, the barrow he circled all without; nor was any there, none in the waste . . .

Yet war he desired, was eager for battle. The barrow he entered, sought the cup, and discovered soon that some one of mortals had searched his treasure, his lordly gold.

The guardian waited ill-enduring till evening came; boiling with wrath was the barrow's keeper, and fain with flame the foe to pay for the dear cup's loss.

—Now day was fled as the worm had wished. By its wall no more was it glad to bide, but burning flew folded in flame: a fearful beginning for sons of the soil; and soon it came, in the doom of their lord, to a dreadful end.

XXXIII

THEN the baleful fiend its fire belched out, and bright homes burned.

The blaze stood high all landsfolk frighting. No living thing would that loathly one leave as aloft it flew.

Wide was the dragon's warring seen, its fiendish fury far and near, as the grim destroyer those Geatish people hated and hounded.

To hidden lair, to its hoard it hastened at hint of dawn.

Folk of the land it had lapped in flame, with bale and brand. In its barrow it trusted, its battling and bulwarks: that boast was vain!

To Beowulf then the bale was told quickly and truly: the king's own home, of buildings the best, in brand-waves melted, that gift-throne of Geats.

To the good old man sad in heart, 'twas heaviest sorrow.

The sage assumed that his sovran God he had angered, breaking ancient law, and embittered the Lord. His breast within with black thoughts welled, as his wont was never.

The folk's own fastness that fiery dragon with flame had destroyed, and the stronghold all washed by waves; but the warlike king, prince of the Weders, plotted vengeance. Warriors'-bulwark, he bade them work all of iron—the earl's commander—a war-shield wondrous: well he knew that forest-wood against fire were worthless, linden could aid not. Atheling brave, he was fated to finish this fleeting life,[1] his days on earth, and the dragon with him, though long it had watched o'er the wealth of the hoard!

Shame he reckoned it, sharer-of-rings, to follow the flyer-afar with a host, a broad-flung band; nor the battle feared he, nor deemed he dreadful the dragon's warring, its vigor and valor: ventures desperate he had passed aplenty, and perils of war, contest-crash, since, conqueror proud, Hrothgar's hall he had wholly purged, and in grapple had killed the kin of Grendel, loathsome breed!

Not least was that of hand-to-hand fights where Hygelac fell, when the ruler of Geats in rush of battle, lord of his folk, in the Frisian land, son of Hrethel, by sword-draughts died, by brands down-beaten.

Thence Beowulf fled through strength of himself and his swimming power, though alone, and his arms were laden with thirty coats of mail, when he came to the sea!

Nor yet might Hetwaras[2] haughtily boast their craft of contest, who carried against him shields to the fight: but few escaped from strife with the hero to seek their homes!

Then swam over ocean Ecgtheow's son lonely and sorrowful, seeking his land, where Hygd made him offer of hoard and realm, rings and royal-seat, reckoning naught the strength of her son to save their kingdom from hostile hordes, after Hygelac's death.

No sooner for this could the stricken ones in any wise move that atheling's mind over young Heardred's head as

---

1. Literally "loan-days," days loaned to man.

2. Chattuarii, a tribe that dwelt along the Rhine, and took part in repelling the raid of (Hygelac) Chocilaicus.

lord and ruler of all the realm to be: yet the hero upheld him with helpful words, aided in honor, till, older grown, he wielded the Weder-Geats.—Wandering exiles sought him o'er seas, the sons of Ohtere, who had spurned the sway of the Scylfings'-helmet, the bravest and best that broke the rings, in Swedish land, of the sea-kings' line, haughty hero.[3]

Hence Heardred's end. For shelter he gave them, sword-death came, the blade's fell blow, to bairn of Hygelac; but the son of Ongentheow sought again house and home when Heardred fell, leaving Beowulf lord of Geats and gift-seat's master.—A good king he!

---

3. Onla, son of Ongentheow, who pursues his two nephews Eanmund and Eadgils to Heardred's court, where they have taken refuge after their unsuccessful rebellion. In the fighting Heardred is killed.

XXXIV

THE fall of his lord he was fain to requite in after days; and to Eadgils he proved friend to the friendless, and forces sent over the sea to the son of Ohtere, weapons and warriors: well repaid he those care-paths cold when the king he slew.[1]

Thus safe through struggles the son of Ecgtheow had passed a plenty, through perils dire, with daring deeds, till this day was come that doomed him now with the dragon to strive.

With comrades eleven the lord of Geats swollen in rage went seeking the dragon. He had heard whence all the harm arose and the killing of clansmen; that cup of price on the lap of the lord had been laid by the finder.

In the throng was this one thirteenth man, starter of all the strife and ill, care-laden captive; cringing thence forced and reluctant, he led them on till he came in ken of that cavern-hall, the barrow delved near billowy surges, flood of ocean.

Within 'twas full of wire-gold and jewels; a jealous warden, warrior trusty, the treasures held, lurked in his lair. Not light the task of entrance for any of earth-born men!

---

1. That is, Beowulf supports Eadgils against Onela, who is slain by Eadgils in revenge for the "care-paths" of exile into which Onela forced him.

Sat on the headland the hero king, spake words of hail to his hearth-companions, gold-friend of Geats. All gloomy his soul, wavering, death-bound.

Wyrd full nigh stood ready to greet the gray-haired man, to seize his soul-hoard, sunder apart life and body. Not long would be the warrior's spirit enwound with flesh.

Beowulf spake, the bairn of Ecgtheow:—

"Through store of struggles I strove in youth, mighty feuds; I mind them all.

I was seven years old when the sovran of rings, friend-of-his-folk, from my father took me, had me, and held me, Hrethel the king, with food and fee, faithful in kinship.

Ne'er, while I lived there, he loathlier found me, bairn in the burg, than his birthright sons, Herebeald and Haethcyn and Hygelac mine.

For the eldest of these, by unmeet chance, by kinsman's deed, was the death-bed strewn, when Haethcyn killed him with horny bow, his own dear liege laid low with an arrow, missed the mark and his mate shot down, one brother the other, with bloody shaft. A feeless fight,[2] and a fearful sin, horror to Hrethel; yet, hard as it was, unavenged must the atheling die!

Too awful it is for an aged man to bide and bear, that his bairn so young rides on the gallows.

A rime he makes, sorrow-song for his son there hanging as rapture of ravens; no rescue now can come from the old, disabled man!

Still is he minded, as morning breaks, of the heir gone elsewhere;[3] another he hopes not he will bide to see his

2. That is, the king could claim no wergild, or man-price, from one son for the killing of the other.

3. Usual euphemism for death.

burg within as ward for his wealth, now the one has found doom of death that the deed incurred.

Forlorn he looks on the lodge of his son, wine-hall waste and wind-swept chambers reft of revel. The rider sleepeth, the hero, far-hidden;[4] no harp resounds, in the courts no wassail, as once was heard.

4. Sc. in the grave.

XXXV

"THEN he goes to his chamber, a grief-song chants alone for his lost. Too large all seems, homestead and house.

So the helmet-of-Weders hid in his heart for Herebeald waves of woe. No way could he take to avenge on the slayer slaughter so foul; nor e'en could he harass that hero at all with loathing deed, though he loved him not.

And so for the sorrow his soul endured, men's gladness he gave up and God's light chose. Lands and cities he left his sons (as the wealthy do) when he went from earth.

There was strife and struggle 'twixt Swede and Geat o'er the width of waters; war arose, hard battle-horror, when Hrethel died, and Ongentheow's offspring grew strife-keen, bold, nor brooked o'er the seas pact of peace, but pushed their hosts to harass in hatred by Hreosnabeorh.

Men of my folk for that feud had vengeance, for woful war ('tis widely known), though one of them bought it with blood of his heart, a bargain hard: for Haethcyn proved fatal that fray, for the first-of-Geats.

At morn, I heard, was the murderer killed by kinsman for kinsman,[1] with clash of sword, when Ongentheow met Eofor there.

---

1. Eofor for Wulf.—The immediate provocation for Eofor in killing "the hoary Scylfing," Ongentheow, is that the latter has just struck Wulf down; but the king, Haethcyn, is also avenged by the blow. See the detailed description below.

Wide split the war-helm: wan he fell, hoary Scylfing; the hand that smote him of feud was mindful, nor flinched from the death-blow.

"For all that he[2] gave me, my gleaming sword repaid him at war,—such power I wielded,—for lordly treasure: with land he entrusted me, homestead and house.

He had no need from Swedish realm, or from Spear-Dane folk, or from men of the Gifths, to get him help,—some warrior worse for wage to buy!

Ever I fought in the front of all, sole to the fore; and so shall I fight while I bide in life and this blade shall last that early and late hath loyal proved since for my doughtiness Daeghrefn fell, slain by my hand, the Hugas' champion.

Nor fared he thence to the Frisian king with the booty back, and breast-adornments; but, slain in struggle, that standard-bearer fell, atheling brave.

Not with blade was he slain, but his bones were broken by brawny gripe, his heart-waves stilled.—The sword-edge now, hard blade and my hand, for the hoard shall strive."

Beowulf spake, and a battle-vow made his last of all: "I have lived through many wars in my youth; now once again, old folk-defender, feud will I seek, do doughty deeds, if the dark destroyer forth from his cavern come to fight me!"

Then hailed he the helmeted heroes all, for the last time greeting his liegemen dear, comrades of war: "I should carry no weapon, no sword to the serpent, if sure I knew how, with such enemy, else my vows I could gain as I did in Grendel's day. But fire in this fight I must fear me

2. Hygelac.

now, and poisonous breath; so I bring with me breastplate and board.[3]

From the barrow's keeper no footbreadth flee I. One fight shall end our war by the wall, as Wyrd allots, all mankind's master.

My mood is bold but forbears to boast o'er this battling-flyer.

—Now abide by the barrow, ye breastplate-mailed, ye heroes in harness, which of us twain better from battle-rush bear his wounds.

Wait ye the finish. The fight is not yours, nor meet for any but me alone to measure might with this monster here and play the hero. Hardily I shall win that wealth, or war shall seize, cruel killing, your king and lord!"

Up stood then with shield the sturdy champion, stayed by the strength of his single manhood, and hardy 'neath helmet his harness bore under cleft of the cliffs: no coward's path!

Soon spied by the wall that warrior chief, survivor of many a victory-field where foemen fought with furious clashings, an arch of stone; and within, a stream that broke from the barrow.

The brooklet's wave was hot with fire. The hoard that way he never could hope unharmed to near, or endure those deeps,[4] for the dragon's flame.

Then let from his breast, for he burst with rage, the Weder-Geat prince a word outgo; stormed the stark-heart; stern went ringing and clear his cry 'neath the cliff-rocks gray.

---

3. Shield.
4. The hollow passage.

The hoard-guard heard a human voice; his rage was enkindled. No respite now for pact of peace!

The poison-breath of that foul worm first came forth from the cave, hot reek-of-fight: the rocks resounded.

Stout by the stone-way his shield he raised, lord of the Geats, against the loathed-one; while with courage keen that coiled foe came seeking strife.

The sturdy king had drawn his sword, not dull of edge, heirloom old; and each of the two felt fear of his foe, though fierce their mood.

Stoutly stood with his shield high-raised the warrior king, as the worm now coiled together amain: the mailed-one waited.

Now, spire by spire, fast sped and glided that blazing serpent.

The shield protected, soul and body a shorter while for the hero-king than his heart desired, could his will have wielded the welcome respite but once in his life!

But Wyrd denied it, and victory's honors.

—His arm he lifted lord of the Geats, the grim foe smote with atheling's heirloom. Its edge was turned brown blade, on the bone, and bit more feebly than its noble master had need of then in his baleful stress.

—Then the barrow's keeper waxed full wild for that weighty blow, cast deadly flames; wide drove and far those vicious fires.

No victor's glory the Geats' lord boasted; his brand had failed, naked in battle, as never it should, excellent iron!

'Twas no easy path that Ecgtheow's honored heir must tread over the plain to the place of the foe; for against his will he must win a home elsewhere far, as must all men, leaving this lapsing life!

—Not long it was ere those champions grimly closed again. The hoard-guard was heartened; high heaved his-breast once more; and by peril was pressed again, enfolded in flames, the folk-commander!

Nor yet about him his band of comrades, sons of athelings, armed stood with warlike front: to the woods they bent them, their lives to save.

But the soul of one with care was cumbered. Kinship true can never be marred in a noble mind!

XXXVI

WIGLAF his name was, Weohstan's son, linden-thane loved, the lord of Scylfings, Aelfhere's kinsman.

His king he now saw with heat under helmet hard oppressed. He minded the prizes his prince had given him, wealthy seat of the Waegmunding line, and folk-rights that his father owned.

Not long he lingered.

The linden yellow, his shield, he seized; the old sword he drew:—as heirloom of Eanmund earth-dwellers knew it, who was slain by the sword-edge, son of Ohtere, friendless exile, erst in fray killed by Weohstan, who won for his kin brown-bright helmet, breastplate ringed, old sword of Eotens, Onela's gift, weeds of war of the warrior-thane, battle-gear brave: though a brother's child had been felled, the feud was unfelt by Onela.[1]

For winters this war-gear Weohstan kept, breastplate and board, till his bairn had grown earlship to earn as the old sire did: then he gave him, mid Geats, the gear of battle, portion huge, when he passed from life, fared aged forth.

---

1. That is, although Eanmund was brother's son to Onela, the slaying of the former by Weohstan is not felt as cause of feud, and is rewarded by gift of the slain man's weapons.

For the first time now with his leader-lord the liegeman young was bidden to share the shock of battle.

Neither softened his soul, nor the sire's bequest weakened in war.[2] So the worm found out when once in fight the foes had met!

Wiglaf spake,—and his words were sage; sad in spirit, he said to his comrades:—

"I remember the time, when mead we took, what promise we made to this prince of ours in the banquet-hall, to our breaker-of-rings, for gear of combat to give him requital, for hard-sword and helmet, if hap should bring stress of this sort!

Himself who chose us from all his army to aid him now, urged us to glory, and gave these treasures, because he counted us keen with the spear and hardy 'neath helm, though this hero-work our leader hoped unhelped and alone to finish for us,—folk-defender who hath got him glory greater than all men for daring deeds!

Now the day is come that our noble master has need of the might of warriors stout. Let us stride along the hero to help while the heat is about him glowing and grim!

For God is my witness I am far more fain the fire should seize along with my lord these limbs of mine![3]

Unsuiting it seems our shields to bear homeward hence, save here we essay to fell the foe and defend the life of the Weders' lord.

---

2. Both Wiglaf and the sword did their duty.—The following is one of the classic passages for illustrating the comitatus as the most conspicuous Germanic institution, and its underlying sense of duty, based partly on the idea of loyalty and partly on the practical basis of benefits received and repaid.

3. Sc. "than to bide safely here,"—a common figure of incomplete comparison.

I wot 'twere shame on the law of our land if alone the king out of Geatish warriors woe endured and sank in the struggle! My sword and helmet, breastplate and board, for us both shall serve!"

Through slaughter-reek strode he to succor his chieftain, his battle-helm bore, and brief words spake:—

"Beowulf dearest, do all bravely, as in youthful days of yore thou vowedst that while life should last thou wouldst let no wise thy glory droop! Now, great in deeds, atheling steadfast, with all thy strength shield thy life! I will stand to help thee."

At the words the worm came once again, murderous monster mad with rage, with fire-billows flaming, its foes to seek, the hated men.

In heat-waves burned that board[4] to the boss, and the breastplate failed to shelter at all the spear-thane young.

Yet quickly under his kinsman's shield went eager the earl, since his own was now all burned by the blaze.

The bold king again had mind of his glory: with might his glaive was driven into the dragon's head,—blow nerved by hate.

But Naegling[5] was shivered, broken in battle was Beowulf's sword, old and gray. 'Twas granted him not that ever the edge of iron at all could help him at strife: too strong was his hand, so the tale is told, and he tried too far with strength of stroke all swords he wielded, though sturdy their steel: they steaded him nought.

Then for the third time thought on its feud that folk-destroyer, fire-dread dragon, and rushed on the hero,

---

4. Wiglaf's wooden shield.

5. Gering would translate "kinsman of the nail," as both are made of iron.

where room allowed, battle-grim, burning; its bitter teeth closed on his neck, and covered him with waves of blood from his breast that welled.

XXXVII

'TWAS now, men say, in his sovran's need that the earl made known his noble strain, craft and keenness and courage enduring. Heedless of harm, though his hand was burned, hardy-hearted, he helped his kinsman.

A little lower the loathsome beast he smote with sword; his steel drove in bright and burnished; that blaze began to lose and lessen.

At last the king wielded his wits again, war-knife drew, a biting blade by his breastplate hanging, and the Weders'-helm smote that worm asunder, felled the foe, flung forth its life.

So had they killed it, kinsmen both, athelings twain: thus an earl should be in danger's day!

Of deeds of valor this conqueror's-hour of the king was last, of his work in the world.

The wound began, which that dragon-of-earth had erst inflicted, to swell and smart; and soon he found in his breast was boiling, baleful and deep, pain of poison.

The prince walked on, wise in his thought, to the wall of rock; then sat, and stared at the structure of giants, where arch of stone and steadfast column upheld forever that hall in earth. Yet here must the hand of the henchman peerless lave with water his winsome lord, the king and conqueror covered with blood, with struggle spent, and unspan his helmet.

Beowulf spake in spite of his hurt, his mortal wound; full well he knew his portion now was past and gone of earthly bliss, and all had fled of his file of days, and death was near:

"I would fain bestow on son of mine this gear of war, were given me now that any heir should after me come of my proper blood. This people I ruled fifty winters. No folk-king was there, none at all, of the neighboring clans who war would wage me with 'warriors'-friends'[1] and threat me with horrors.

At home I bided what fate might come, and I cared for mine own; feuds I sought not, nor falsely swore ever on oath.

For all these things, though fatally wounded, fain am I!

From the Ruler-of-Man no wrath shall seize me, when life from my frame must flee away, for killing of kinsmen!

Now quickly go and gaze on that hoard 'neath the hoary rock, Wiglaf loved, now the worm lies low, sleeps, heart-sore, of his spoil bereaved. And fare in haste. I would fain behold the gorgeous heirlooms, golden store, have joy in the jewels and gems, lay down softlier for sight of this splendid hoard my life and the lordship I long have held."

---

1. That is, swords.

XXXVIII

I HAVE heard that swiftly the son of Weohstan at wish and word of his wounded king,—war-sick warrior,—woven mail-coat, battle-sark, bore 'neath the barrow's roof.

Then the clansman keen, of conquest proud, passing the seat,[1] saw store of jewels and glistening gold the ground along; by the wall were marvels, and many a vessel in the den of the dragon, the dawn-flier old: unburnished bowls of bygone men reft of richness; rusty helms of the olden age; and arm-rings many wondrously woven.—Such wealth of gold, booty from barrow, can burden with pride each human wight: let him hide it who will!—

His glance too fell on a gold-wove banner high o'er the hoard, of handiwork noblest, brilliantly broidered; so bright its gleam, all the earth-floor he easily saw and viewed all these vessels.

No vestige now was seen of the serpent: the sword had ta'en him.

Then, I heard, the hill of its hoard was reft, old work of giants, by one alone; he burdened his bosom with beakers and plate at his own good will, and the ensign took, brightest of beacons.—The blade of his lord—its edge was iron—had injured deep one that guarded the golden hoard many

1. Where Beowulf lay.

a year and its murder-fire spread hot round the barrow in horror-billows at midnight hour, till it met its doom.

Hasted the herald, the hoard so spurred him his track to retrace; he was troubled by doubt, high-souled hero, if haply he'd find alive, where he left him, the lord of Weders, weakening fast by the wall of the cave.

So he carried the load. His lord and king he found all bleeding, famous chief at the lapse of life.

The liegeman again plashed him with water, till point of word broke through the breast-hoard.

Beowulf spake, sage and sad, as he stared at the gold.—

"For the gold and treasure, to God my thanks, to the Wielder-of-Wonders, with words I say, for what I behold, to Heaven's Lord, for the grace that I give such gifts to my folk or ever the day of my death be run!

Now I've bartered here for booty of treasure the last of my life, so look ye well to the needs of my land! No longer I tarry.

A barrow bid ye the battle-fanned raise for my ashes. 'Twill shine by the shore of the flood, to folk of mine memorial fair on Hrones Headland high uplifted, that ocean-wanderers oft may hail Beowulf's Barrow, as back from far they drive their keels o'er the darkling wave."

From his neck he unclasped the collar of gold, valorous king, to his vassal gave it with bright-gold helmet, breastplate, and ring, to the youthful thane: bade him use them in joy.

"Thou art end and remnant of all our race the Waegmunding name. For Wyrd hath swept them, all my line, to the land of doom, earls in their glory: I after them go."

This word was the last which the wise old man harbored in heart ere hot death-waves of balefire he chose. From his bosom fled his soul to seek the saints' reward.

XXXIX

IT was heavy hap for that hero young on his lord beloved to look and find him lying on earth with life at end, sorrowful sight.

But the slayer too, awful earth-dragon, empty of breath, lay felled in fight, nor, fain of its treasure, could the writhing monster rule it more. For edges of iron had ended its days, hard and battle-sharp, hammers' leaving;[1] and that flier-afar had fallen to ground hushed by its hurt, its hoard all near, no longer lusty aloft to whirl at midnight, making its merriment seen, proud of its prizes: prone it sank by the handiwork of the hero-king.

Forsooth among folk but few achieve,—though sturdy and strong, as stories tell me, and never so daring in deed of valor,—the perilous breath of a poison-foe to brave, and to rush on the ring-board hall, whenever his watch the warden keeps bold in the barrow.

Beowulf paid the price of death for that precious hoard; and each of the foes had found the end of this fleeting life.

Befell erelong that the laggards in war the wood had left, trothbreakers, cowards, ten together, fearing before to flourish a spear in the sore distress of their sovran lord. Now in their shame their shields they carried, armor of fight, where the old man lay; and they gazed on Wiglaf.

---

1. What had been left or made by the hammer; well-forged.

Wearied he sat at his sovran's shoulder, shieldsman good, to wake him with water.[2]

Nowise it availed. Though well he wished it, in world no more could he barrier life for that leader-of-battles nor baffle the will of all-wielding God. Doom of the Lord was law o'er the deeds of every man, as it is to-day.

Grim was the answer, easy to get, from the youth for those that had yielded to fear!

Wiglaf spake, the son of Weohstan,—mournful he looked on those men unloved:—

"Who sooth will speak, can say indeed that the ruler who gave you golden rings and the harness of war in which ye stand—for he at ale-bench often-times bestowed on hall-folk helm and breastplate, lord to liegemen, the likeliest gear which near of far he could find to give,—threw away and wasted these weeds of battle, on men who failed when the foemen came!

Not at all could the king of his comrades-in-arms venture to vaunt, though the Victory-Wielder, God, gave him grace that he got revenge sole with his sword in stress and need.

To rescue his life, 'twas little that I could serve him in struggle; yet shift I made (hopeless it seemed) to help my kinsman. Its strength ever waned, when with weapon I struck that fatal foe, and the fire less strongly flowed from its head.—Too few the heroes in throe of contest that thronged to our king!

Now gift of treasure and girding of sword, joy of the house and home-delight shall fail your folk; his freehold-land every clansman within your kin shall lose and leave,

---

2. Trying to revive him.

when lords highborn hear afar of that flight of yours, a fameless deed.

Yea, death is better for liegemen all than a life of shame!”

XL

THAT battle-toil bade he at burg to announce, at the fort on the cliff, where, full of sorrow, all the morning earls had sat, daring shieldsmen, in doubt of twain: would they wail as dead, or welcome home, their lord beloved?

Little[1] kept back of the tidings new, but told them all, the herald that up the headland rode.—

"Now the willing-giver to Weder folk in death-bed lies; the Lord of Geats on the slaughter-bed sleeps by the serpent's deed! And beside him is stretched that slayer-of-men with knife-wounds sick:[2] no sword availed on the awesome thing in any wise to work a wound.

There Wiglaf sitteth, Weohstan's bairn, by Beowulf's side, the living earl by the other dead, and heavy of heart a head-watch[3] keeps o'er friend and foe.—Now our folk may look for waging of war when once unhidden to Frisian and Frank the fall of the king is spread afar.—The strife began when hot on the Hugas[4] Hygelac fell and fared with his fleet to the Frisian land.

Him there the Hetwaras humbled in war, plied with such prowess their power o'erwhelming that the bold-in-battle bowed beneath it and fell in fight.

1. Nothing.
2. Dead.
3. Death-watch, guard of honor, "lyke-wake."
4. A name for the Franks.

To his friends no wise could that earl give treasure! And ever since the Merowings' favor has failed us wholly.

Nor aught expect I of peace and faith from Swedish folk. 'Twas spread afar how Ongentheow reft at Ravenswood Haethcyn Hrethling of hope and life, when the folk of Geats for the first time sought in wanton pride the Warlike-Scylfings. Soon the sage old sire[5] of Ohtere, ancient and awful, gave answering blow; the sea-king[6] he slew, and his spouse redeemed, his good wife rescued, though robbed of her gold, mother of Ohtere and Onela.

Then he followed his foes, who fled before him sore beset and stole their way, bereft of a ruler, to Ravenswood. With his host he besieged there what swords had left, the weary and wounded; woes he threatened the whole night through to that hard-pressed throng: some with the morrow his sword should kill, some should go to the gallows-tree for rapture of ravens.

But rescue came with dawn of day for those desperate men when they heard the horn of Hygelac sound, tones of his trumpet; the trusty king had followed their trail with faithful band.

5. Ongentheow
6. Haethcyn

XLI

"THE bloody swath of Swedes and Geats and the storm of their strife, were seen afar, how folk against folk the fight had wakened.

The ancient king with his atheling band sought his citadel, sorrowing much: Ongentheow earl went up to his burg.

He had tested Hygelac's hardihood, the proud one's prowess, would prove it no longer, defied no more those fighting-wanderers nor hoped from the seamen to save his hoard, his bairn and his bride: so he bent him again, old, to his earth-walls.

Yet after him came with slaughter for Swedes the standards of Hygelac o'er peaceful plains in pride advancing, till Hrethelings fought in the fenced town.[1]

Then Ongentheow with edge of sword, the hoary-bearded, was held at bay, and the folk-king there was forced to suffer Eofor's anger.

In ire, at the king Wulf Wonreding with weapon struck; and the chieftain's blood, for that blow, in streams flowed 'neath his hair. No fear felt he, stout old Scylfing, but

1. The line may mean: till Hrethelings stormed on the hedged shields,— i.e. the shield-wall or hedge of defensive war— Hrethelings, of course, are Geats.

straightway repaid in better bargain that bitter stroke and faced his foe with fell intent.

Nor swift enough was the son of Wonred answer to render the aged chief; too soon on his head the helm was cloven; blood-bedecked he bowed to earth, and fell adown; not doomed was he yet, and well he waxed, though the wound was sore.

Then the hardy Hygelac-thane,[2] when his brother fell, with broad brand smote, giants' sword crashing through giants'-helm across the shield-wall: sank the king, his folk's old herdsman, fatally hurt.

There were many to bind the brother's wounds and lift him, fast as fate allowed his people to wield the place-of-war. But Eofor took from Ongentheow, earl from other, the iron-breastplate, hard sword hilted, and helmet too, and the hoar-chief's harness to Hygelac carried, who took the trappings, and truly promised rich fee 'mid folk,—and fulfilled it so.

For that grim strife gave the Geatish lord, Hrethel's offspring, when home he came, to Eofor and Wulf a wealth of treasure: Each of them had a hundred thousand[3] in land and linked rings; nor at less price reckoned mid-earth men such mighty deeds! And to Eofor he gave his only daughter in pledge of grace, the pride of his home.

"Such is the feud, the foeman's rage, death-hate of men: so I deem it sure that the Swedish folk will seek us home for this fall of their friends, the fighting-Scylfings, when once they learn that our warrior leader lifeless lies, who land and hoard ever defended from all his foes, furthered

---

2. Eofor, brother to Wulf Wonreding.
3. Sc. "value in" hides and the weight of the gold.

his folk's weal, finished his course a hardy hero.—Now haste is best, that we go to gaze on our Geatish lord, and bear the bountiful breaker-of-rings to the funeral pyre.

No fragments merely shall burn with the warrior. Wealth of jewels, gold untold and gained in terror, treasure at last with his life obtained, all of that booty the brands shall take, fire shall eat it.

No earl must carry memorial jewel. No maiden fair shall wreathe her neck with noble ring: nay, sad in spirit and shorn of her gold, oft shall she pass o'er paths of exile now our lord all laughter has laid aside, all mirth and revel.

Many a spear morning-cold shall be clasped amain, lifted aloft; nor shall lilt of harp those warriors wake; but the wan-hued raven, fain o'er the fallen, his feast shall praise and boast to the eagle how bravely he ate when he and the wolf were wasting the slain."

So he told his sorrowful tidings, and little[4] he lied, the loyal man of word or of work.

The warriors rose; sad, they climbed to the Cliff-of-Eagles, went, welling with tears, the wonder to view.

Found on the sand there, stretched at rest, their lifeless lord, who had lavished rings of old upon them.

Ending-day had dawned on the doughty-one; death had seized in woful slaughter the Weders' king. There saw they, besides, the strangest being, loathsome, lying their leader near, prone on the field.

The fiery dragon, fearful fiend, with flame was scorched. Reckoned by feet, it was fifty measures in length as it lay.

---

4. Not at all.

Aloft erewhile it had revelled by night, and anon come back, seeking its den; now in death's sure clutch it had come to the end of its earth-hall joys.

By it there stood the stoups and jars; dishes lay there, and dear-decked swords eaten with rust, as, on earth's lap resting, a thousand winters they waited there. For all that heritage huge, that gold of bygone men, was bound by a spell,[5] so the treasure-hall could be touched by none of human kind,—save that Heaven's King, God himself, might give whom he would, Helper of Heroes, the hoard to open,—even such a man as seemed to him meet.

5. Laid on it when it was put in the barrow. This spell, or in our days the "curse," either prevented discovery or brought dire ills on the finder and taker.

XLII

A PERILOUS path, it proved, he[1] trod who heinously hid, that hall within, wealth under wall! Its watcher had killed one of a few,[2] and the feud was avenged in woful fashion.

Wondrous seems it, what manner a man of might and valor oft ends his life, when the earl no longer in mead-hall may live with loving friends.

So Beowulf, when that barrow's warden he sought, and the struggle; himself knew not in what wise he should wend from the world at last. For[3] princes potent, who placed the gold, with a curse to doomsday covered it deep, so that marked with sin the man should be, hedged with horrors, in hell-bonds fast, racked with plagues, who should rob their hoard.

Yet no greed for gold, but the grace of heaven, ever the king had kept in view.[4]

---

1. Probably the fugitive is meant who discovered the hoard. Ten Brink and Gering assume that the dragon is meant. "Hid" may well mean here "took while in hiding."

2. That is "one and a few others." But Beowulf seems to be indicated.

3. Ten Brink points out the strongly heathen character of this part of the epic. Beowulf's end came, so the old tradition ran, from his unwitting interference with spell-bound treasure.

4. A hard saying, variously interpreted. In any case, it is the somewhat clumsy effort of the Christian poet to tone down the heathenism of his material by an edifying observation.

Wiglaf spake, the son of Weohstan:—

"At the mandate of one, oft warriors many sorrow must suffer; and so must we.

The people's-shepherd showed not aught of care for our counsel, king beloved!

That guardian of gold he should grapple not, urged we, but let him lie where he long had been in his earth-hall waiting the end of the world, the hest of heaven.—This hoard is ours but grievously gotten; too grim the fate which thither carried our king and lord.

I was within there, and all I viewed, the chambered treasure, when chance allowed me (and my path was made in no pleasant wise) under the earth-wall. Eager, I seized such heap from the hoard as hands could bear and hurriedly carried it hither back to my liege and lord.

Alive was he still, still wielding his wits. The wise old man spake much in his sorrow, and sent you greetings and bade that ye build, when he breathed no more, on the place of his balefire a barrow high, memorial mighty.

Of men was he worthiest warrior wide earth o'er the while he had joy of his jewels and burg.

Let us set out in haste now, the second time to see and search this store of treasure, these wall-hid wonders,—the way I show you,—where, gathered near, ye may gaze your fill at broad-gold and rings.

Let the bier, soon made, be all in order when out we come, our king and captain to carry thither—man beloved—where long he shall bide safe in the shelter of sovran God."

Then the bairn of Weohstan bade command, hardy chief, to heroes many that owned their homesteads, hither to bring firewood from far—o'er the folk they ruled—for the famed-one's funeral.

"Fire shall devour and wan flames feed on the fearless warrior who oft stood stout in the iron-shower, when, sped from the string, a storm of arrows shot o'er the shield-wall: the shaft held firm, featly feathered, followed the barb."

And now the sage young son of Weohstan seven chose of the chieftain's thanes, the best he found that band within, and went with these warriors, one of eight, under hostile roof. In hand one bore a lighted torch and led the way.

No lots they cast for keeping the hoard when once the warriors saw it in hall, altogether without a guardian, lying there lost. And little they mourned when they had hastily haled it out, dear-bought treasure!

The dragon they cast, the worm, o'er the wall for the wave to take, and surges swallowed that shepherd of gems.

Then the woven gold on a wain was laden—countless quite!—and the king was borne, hoary hero, to Hrones-Ness.

XLIII

THEN fashioned for him the folk of Geats firm on the earth a funeral-pile, and hung it with helmets and harness of war and breastplates bright, as the boon he asked; and they laid amid it the mighty chieftain, heroes mourning their master dear.

Then on the hill that hugest of balefires the warriors wakened.

Wood-smoke rose black over blaze, and blent was the roar of flame with weeping (the wind was still), till the fire had broken the frame of bones, hot at the heart.

heavy mood their misery moaned they, their master's death. Wailing her woe, the widow[1] old, her hair upbound, for Beowulf's death sung in her sorrow, and said full oft she dreaded the doleful days to come, deaths enow, and doom of battle, and shame.—The smoke by the sky was devoured.

The folk of the Weders fashioned there on the headland a barrow broad and high, by ocean-farers far descried: in ten days' time their toil had raised it, the battle-brave's beacon.

1. Nothing is said of Beowulf's wife in the poem, but Bugge surmises that Beowulf finally accepted Hygd's offer of kingdom and hoard, and, as was usual, took her into the bargain.

Round brands of the pyre a wall they built, the worthiest ever that wit could prompt in their wisest men.

They placed in the barrow that precious booty, the rounds and the rings they had reft erewhile, hardy heroes, from hoard in cave,—trusting the ground with treasure of earls, gold in the earth, where ever it lies useless to men as of yore it was.

Then about that barrow the battle-keen rode, atheling-born, a band of twelve, lament to make, to mourn their king, chant their dirge, and their chieftain honor.

They praised his earlship, his acts of prowess worthily witnessed: and well it is that men their master-friend mightily laud, heartily love, when hence he goes from life in the body forlorn away.

Thus made their mourning the men of Geatland, for their hero's passing his hearth-companions: quoth that of all the kings of earth, of men he was mildest and most beloved, to his kin the kindest, keenest for praise.

www.ingramcontent.com/pod-product-compliance
Lightning Source LLC
Chambersburg PA
CBHW030414310726
48979CB00002B/405
9781434115249